PRAISE FOR
RON FAUST

"Sheer suspense!"

—*Booklist*

"Faust's prose is as smooth and bright as a sunlit mirror."

—*Publishers Weekly*

"Hemingway is alive and well and writing under the name Ron Faust."

—Ed Gorman, author of *Night Kills*

"Faust is one of our heavyweights . . . you can't read a book by Ron Faust without the phrase 'major motion picture' coming to mind."

—Dean Ing, *New York Times* bestselling author of *The Ransom of Black Stealth One*

"Faust writes of nature and men like Hemingway, with simplicity and absolute dominance of prose skills."

—Bill Granger, award-winning author of *Hemingway's Notebook*

"He looms head and shoulders above them all—truly the master storyteller of our time. Faust will inevitably be compared to Hemingway."

—Robert Bloch, author of *Psycho*

ALSO BY RON FAUST

Jackstraw

Snowkill

The Burning Sky

The Long Count

Death Fires

Nowhere to Run

THE WOLF IN THE CLOUDS

RON FAUST

TURNER

Turner Publishing Company
200 4th Avenue North • Suite 950 • Nashville, Tennessee 37219
445 Park Avenue • 9th Floor • New York, New York 10022

www.turnerpublishing.com

THE WOLF IN THE CLOUDS

This is a work of fiction. All the characters and events portrayed in this book are either products of the author's imagination or are used fictitiously.

Cover design: Glen M. Edelstein
Book design: Glen M. Edelstein

Library of Congress Catalog-in-Publishing Data
Faust, Ron.
The wolf in the clouds / Ron Faust.
pages ; cm.
ISBN 978-1-62045-426-8
I. Title.
PS3556.A98W65 2013
813'.54--dc23

2013005076

Printed in the United States of America
13 14 15 16 17 18 19 0 9 8 7 6 5 4 3 2 1

"BITCH WHORE SLUT, TAKE OFF YOUR CLOTHES"

Karen Bright pulled her hand from mine and began undressing. She removed her jacket, her sweater, a turtleneck jersey, her bra. She was crying. She moved slowly, with shaky coordination. Weeping, she bent over and unzipped her gaiters, unlaced and removed her boots, then pulled down her ski pants. When the pants were around her ankles, she slipped and fell on the floor. She finished removing her ski pants and then, without rising, pulled off her long underwear bottoms. She sat on the floor and wept quietly.

Ralph had established his dominance; he had, in a real way, hypnotized her. She had surrendered her mind and body to him. I could feel my own self going, too, leaking out of me. It would be so easy to surrender completely. I hoped that I could at least avert the final horror of collaborating with my murderer. When the time came, I wanted to run, shouting defiantly, in the muzzle of his rifle . . .

THE WOLF IN THE CLOUDS

ONE

My sleep was shallow and I awakened before the alarm was due to ring. The luminous green hands of the clock horizontally bisected the dial—a quarter to three. The ticking sounded loud in this abnormal silence.

The propane had run out during the night and the house was very cold: when I turned on the small bedside lamp I could see my breath emerge in pale clouds of vapor. Jan was annoyed by the light; she grimaced, moaned a soft bubbly complaint, and turned over.

The window was frosted into a white fern jungle. I held my palm against the frost until a spot melted, then leaned close and looked outside. It was a hushed and frozen night, all blacks and grays and whites, planes and angles, nature in a geometrical mood. There did not seem to be any wind now. And it had finally stopped snowing. I looked up through the tangle of cottonwood branches, but I could not see the moon or the stars. The snow seemed to possess its own illumination.

I went into the living room and got dressed. First the suit of woolen underwear, then long cotton stockings, and over them heavy woolen stockings that came above my knees; garters, and then the wool knickers, stitched and patched and worn smooth after all the years. Now the knee-length gaiters, a loose cashmere sweater with holes in the elbows, a wool shirt, and finally my down jacket. I sat and laced my boots. They had been resoled twice and the leather uppers were cracked and scuffed, but the boots were warm and fit me like a second skin. I stood up. I was warm now, though perhaps later no amount of clothing could defeat the cold.

My skis and the bamboo poles were leaning against the wall. The poles were made of good quality Tonkin cane; the skis were a compromise between the very light and fragile Nordic touring skis and the heavier, stronger ski-mountaineering type. They were 57 mm wide, with a hickory sole, lignostone edges, and the Silvretta Saas-Fee binding. Technically, the equipment was the property of the U.S. Forest Service. In every other way but technically, they were mine. I used them to go far back in the mountains to measure the depth and moisture content of the snow at various points in the Wolf Basin watershed. It was good winter duty. Better, anyway, than sitting at a desk in an overheated office, or giving Smokey the Bear talks to grammar school students.

My other gear was spread out over the floor. There was my big rucksack, once a smoky gray and now stained to a mottled brown, a down sleeping bag, the little Svea stove, kettles, fuel, water bottles, food, additional clothing, odds and ends.

I went into the kitchen and placed a pot of coffee on the electric stove. While the water was heating I went outside for some piñon logs. It was a night of cold and menace. The cold was light, dry, intense. It was so cold that it seemed the opposite, as dry ice is so cold in the hand that it burns. My teeth and lungs ached. My breath steamed. The snow was granular in this cold, like sand, and made a sound like sand being compressed underfoot. The white aspens and the darker cottonwoods were crucified against a septic sky. Nothing, not even the hoot of an owl or the howl of a dog, challenged the brittle cold silence. Something about this night stabbed into a primitive part of the mind. Fear was the natural response.

There was a mercury thermometer above the woodpile: twenty-seven degrees below zero. We were at 8,500 feet. Roughly figuring a temperature drop of three degrees for each thousand feet of altitude, it was now around forty degrees below zero in the cirque beneath Mt. Wolf. The wind would roar and scream like jet engines up there. That wind could kill you in a couple of hours. I hoped the college kids had been lucky and found the Columbine Cabin during the storm. They were too green to survive without good shelter. I hoped they had found the cabin, and I hoped equally that Ralph Brace had not.

I brushed snow off the woodpile. The logs were frozen solidly together in an ice-glazed mass that looked like petrified wood. They were nearly as hard, too, but with the ax and a crowbar I managed to extract three of the large split logs. The chopping sounds were dulled, absorbed by the snow and the night. My fingers were stiff and without feeling by the time I had finished.

In the fireplace, a few orange coals still glowed beneath the powdery gray ash. I fed the coals some newspaper, a few sticks of dry kindling wood, and then the icy logs. The logs hissed and steamed. The raw ax scars took fire first, then the bark, and then the logs thawed and began burning evenly. The house was now filled with the perfumed scent of piñon and the heavier, darker smell of brewing coffee.

I went into the kitchen and poured a cup of coffee. It was hot and strong and bitter. I lit a cigarette and sat quietly, smoking, drinking the coffee, worrying. I poured an ounce of brandy into the second cup. I was awake now and not altogether happy with that state.

I thought about gem-clear blue water, white sand beaches so hot they burned the soles of your feet, a brutal atomic sun which filled the sky from horizon to horizon. Sun, heat, languor, some fishing, maybe a little skin diving, lots of fresh seafood, and cases and cases of Bohemia and Dos Equis beer. No snow, no tree-splitting cold. My vacation was due in ten days, and we were going to Mexico. I looked forward to complaining about the heat. Mosquitoes. Jan telling me that sweat was ruining my sport shirts. Sunburned, whining children.

The fire in the other room was humming and crackling now, but the house did not seem to be getting warmer. I had heard Jan moving around in the bedroom, and now heard the door open and soon after that a soft, throaty moan. It sounded like the despairing moan of a small predator-surprised animal. I got up and went into the living room. Jan was standing in front of the fireplace, knees bent, shoulders hunched, arms hugging herself. She wore wool slacks and a bulky knit sweater. Her dark blond hair fell down past her shoulders in a silky cascade. Jan was not beautiful, but her hair sometimes made her appear so. Now red firelight moved over her hair and tinted her skin.

"You didn't have to get up," I said.

She turned. "Oh, God, Jack, I'm so *cold.*"

"The cold is bracing."

"I hope that isn't a pun."

"The propane ran out last night."

"Jack, I told you last week to have the tank filled."

"The fire will warm you."

"The fire will blister my front while my rear stays frozen."

I moved closer. Heat from the fire radiated several feet into the room and was then turned back by the cold. "You can always toast the other side," I said.

"I'd better look in on the kids."

"They're okay. They have plenty of blankets."

She turned so that her back was to the fire. "Are you going to bring in more wood?"

"Yes."

"Just bring in enough to last until eight-thirty or nine. I'll call the gas company then."

"All right."

"Jack, really, why don't you get us transferred away from here? To where it's warm?"

"Where to? Florida, Arizona? California—how about Death Valley?"

"No, I'm serious."

"This is a good place, Jan."

"The Virgin Islands would be nice."

"They certainly would. And I could probably get shifted there if your father were a powerful senator or Secretary of the Interior. Anyway, there's a kind of Mau Mau thing going on down there."

"Hawaii, then."

"That's easy," I said. "No one wants to work in Hawaii."

"Where is Frank?" Jan asked.

"He'll be along soon."

"How long are you going to be gone?"

"I don't know, Jan. A day and a half at the most. But I'll probably be home tonight."

"Is it going to be dangerous?"

"No. In and out."

"What about Ralph Brace?"

"I'm sure Ralph is hanging around the ski area. He's fifteen miles from the Columbine."

"How do you know that?"

"Anyway, I always got along well with Ralph, and so did Frank. He wouldn't hurt us."

"Oh, Jack, for God's sake, Jack!" Jan said. "Mrs. Fielding always got along with Ralph, too, and she's dead."

"I know, I know. He's a mad dog."

"I didn't say that."

"Look, Jan, I liked Ralph. Okay. It may sound weird, but I liked him yesterday morning and I like him *this* morning, even though he went berserk in between. Maybe tomorrow I can hate him—I don't know."

"You know what I mean," she said.

"Do you want some coffee?"

"Yes. How much did it snow last night?"

"About eighteen inches down here."

"And up high? Where you're going?"

"Probably three, three and a half feet of new snow."

"Jack, I don't care what you say, it's dangerous. All that snow up there and this terrible cold. Not to mention darling Ralph. It's really not your job. They can't make you do it. You can refuse and no one will say anything."

"Come on."

We went into the kitchen and Jan poured herself a mug of coffee. She said it tasted like rotten acorns. I poured the last of the brandy into her cup, and then she said it tasted like rotten acorns with turpentine. Her face was very pale, and the darkness of her eyebrows and the clean dark blue of her eyes were accentuated. She shivered. Her breasts were free under the heavy sweater. There were freckles on the backs of her hands.

"What is the temperature?" she asked.

"You don't want to know."

"Jack . . ."

"Twenty-seven below."

"Oh, God," she said. She got up from the table and went to the stove. She greased a skillet and placed it over one of the burners. "Jack. I dreamed about those young people all night."

"Yes?"

"Do you think they're still alive?"

"If they found the shelter."

"Well, do you think they found it?"

"No."

"Then why are you going up there?"

"Because we have to try."

She sliced four strips of bacon from the slab and spread them into the skillet. Her head was lowered, and a dark gold wing of hair fell forward and obscured her face.

"But you really think they're dead."

"We have to act as if they're alive."

"You don't think they could find the cabin?"

"Not in that storm. But I don't know; they might have lucked out."

"Jack, you and Frank are almost glad for this opportunity, aren't you? You're turning it into sport."

"That isn't true."

"It's an adventure."

"Jan. If you think I can get any sport out of the suffering of three—hell, four—people, then we understand each other less than I thought."

"Don't twist my meanings that way."

"Well, what is it that you mean?"

"I mean—I don't know." She cleared her throat. "I'm sorry. I hate to be bitchy. But everything feels wrong about this. I'm scared, Jack, really I am."

"It's confused," I said.

"Yes. Well, why don't you go out and get some more wood for me while I cook your breakfast?"

"Okay. If you'll turn down the rheostat on your feminine intuition."

TWO

I went outside and the moisture froze in my nostrils. When I breathed through my mouth there was a catch in the lungs; it was like breathing ammonia or chlorine gas.

The night had not changed: the tree branches were a confused, delicate tracery against the blackness; the snow shone palely, from within; the silence was so complete that all I heard was a ringing in my ears, like the hushed music in a seashell. I had the feeling that everything was made of brittle glass. The air, the sky, the trees, the house, myself—we were all glass and about to shatter. Cold had crystallized the world.

Again I had to chop logs free of the woodpile. I had five of them spread out on the snow when I heard a car engine. It was running roughly in this cold. The sound grew louder; then bright lights arced through the trees, briefly illuminating them and the house. It was Treblene. The jeep station wagon came slowly down the driveway, tire chains clattering with an ugly metallic dissonance. The jeep stopped a few yards away. The engine died and the lights were turned off. I could see very little now after the glare. The car door slammed, and the shadow of a man, outlined by a thin violet aura, came toward me. The snow crunched dryly.

"A bitter night," Treblene said.

"Twenty-seven below," I said.

"Thirty below at my place. And I think it's going to snow some more."

"I doubt it."

"I can smell it."

"It's too cold to snow now," I said. My eyes had partly readjusted to the darkness, but I still could not see him clearly. He was just a shadow, and his face was a pale, featureless oval. His eyeglasses glinted with tiny crescents of light.

"Frank," I said, "maybe we ought to call this off."

"Why?"

"Because those kids are dead."

"Maybe not, Jack."

"Sure they are. They couldn't find the cabin in that storm. It has to be nearly forty below zero up there, and the wind would cut you in half."

"Not necessarily. It could be calm."

"Frank."

"Anyway, it's probably warmer up near the Wolf than it is here. We've got a temperature inversion."

"Even so . . ."

Treblene was silent for a moment. "Look, I give them a twenty percent chance of stumbling into the cabin. Hell, thirty percent."

"The cabin hasn't been used since September. It's just a snowdrift now. They could ski right over the top of it and never know."

"Jack, *someone* has to go up there and look for them."

"Sure. Send a helicopter. They could search the whole basin in the time it would take us to simply reach the area."

"It might not clear up."

"Okay. Now why don't you go into the house and have a cup of coffee while I finish with the wood."

"I'll help you with it."

"Go talk to Jan. She's feeling intuitive."

"I know what you mean." He paused thoughtfully for a while, wanting to speak, but then he turned and went through the snow to the door.

I hacked a few more logs free of the woodpile and in two trips carried all of them inside the house. The room was warmer now, or maybe it just seemed so because I had been outdoors for fifteen minutes. I prodded the fire with an old ski pole I used for a poker and then placed a new log on the fire.

Treblene and Jan were sitting at the kitchen table. Frank's glasses had steamed over and he'd removed them. His eyes looked small and rather vague without the glasses. He was very nearsighted. Now he looked as if he half-expected a blow to originate somewhere out in the blurriness. He squinted at me.

"What did you decide?" he asked.

I pulled out a chair and sat down. "I'm not going."

He looked at me and then turned away. "All right."

"I think you should go, Jack," my wife said.

"A few minutes ago you believed I shouldn't go."

"I know, but Frank here thinks there's a chance. If there is the slightest hope, then you should go up there. You're needed."

"Jesus Christ," I said. I got up, went to the stove and poured a cup of coffee.

"Your breakfast is warming in the oven," Jan said.

I carried the coffee and the plate with three eggs, bacon, potatoes and toast over to the table and started eating. They tried to find some neutral place to look while I ate. I finished the last triangle of toast, drank the coffee and then patted my pockets.

"Here," Frank said, offering me his package of cigarettes.

I withdrew two cigarettes, gave one to Jan, and struck a match. She inhaled, drawing the smoke all the way down and holding it there until, when she finally exhaled, the smoke was hardly visible. Jan had a suicidal way of smoking.

"Well?" she asked.

"Okay."

"Okay what?"

"Okay I'll go."

"I'll heat some water so you can shave," Jan said.

"Let it go."

"But you haven't shaved since Friday. You look like a pirate. Doesn't he look like a pirate, Frank?"

"The worst kind of pirate," Treblene said.

"A bullied pirate," I said. "I'll shave when we get back. Or maybe I'll grow a beard this winter."

"You will not," Jan said.

I stood up. "I suppose we should get going. Have you looked through my gear, Frank?"

"No. Should I?"

"No sense in doubling up on stuff."

We all went into the living room.

"I've got a Primus," Frank said.

"Two stoves won't hurt," I said. "And they're light."

"Do you have sunglasses?"

"Yes."

"What about an ice ax, Jack?"

"I can't see how we'll be getting into ice."

Treblene nodded.

"What do you have in your medical kit?" I asked.

"The usual."

"Drugs?"

"Benzedrine, Roniacol, Darvon."

"Coramine?"

"Coramine, yeah."

"Morphine?"

"No."

"Let's see if we can get some morphine, Frank. What have you got in the way of ski waxes?"

"Everything we'll need."

Jan was watching us. "Is it going to be dangerous?" she asked.

"Not a bit, Jan," Frank said.

"What about avalanches?" she said.

Frank grinned. "Jack can smell an avalanche three counties away."

"You could, too," I said, "if you'd been buried under one."

Frank was still grinning. "Jack worries about avalanches when he goes into the refrigerator for a beer. Jack starts sweating when he sees frost on the lawn. No, Jan, you don't have to worry about avalanches."

I packed my rucksack and carried it outside. Frank carried my skis and poles. As we started down the driveway I remembered that I had left my camera behind. I was a fair amateur photographer; *Colorado* magazine and the *Denver Post* had accepted a few of my mountain pictures, and I figured that if the sun came out today I might have an opportunity for some spectacular shots.

I returned to the house. Jan was standing close to the fire. She turned. "Did you forget something?"

"My camera."

"Tourist."

I looked through the bedroom and then the den, but I could not find my photography equipment. I went back into the living room.

"Jan, where is my camera satchel?"

"I don't—oh, wait. I'm sorry, Jack. Scotty was playing with it in the kids' room yesterday."

"What? Jan, you mean that you permitted that little vandal to play with my three-hundred-dollar camera?"

"I watched him very carefully, Jack."

"You watched him."

"He didn't hurt anything. I took the things away from him after a few minutes and put them on the top shelf of the closet."

"My God," I said, staring at her. "Do you want me to tie your shoes before I go?"

She turned back to the fire.

"There's a point, Jan, where innocence becomes slovenly and fey. You're too old to be a fairy or a troll. The children are turning into wild beasts. Mind my words, Jan, someday they'll be cracking our thigh bones for marrow."

I went into the children's bedroom, hit the light switch and got my camera and two rolls of film from the satchel on the closet shelf. The camera had been lubricated with a special oil, so perhaps the cold would not freeze the mechanism. I hung the camera around my neck and tucked it inside the down jacket; body warmth should keep it functioning.

There were lumps beneath the blankets on the twin beds. The lumps swelled, deflated, expanded again. Scotty and Susan. Hansel and Gretel. Bonnie and Clyde. Odd: I favored Scotty, while Jan always seemed to identify with Susan. Narcissus leading Oedipus in the early innings.

"I don't care what you do with your lives," I said. "Just stay out of the U.S. Congress." I returned to the living room.

"Be careful, Jack," Jan said.

"Sure. Always."

"Are the kids all right?"

"Weird," I said. "They've turned into mushrooms, giant morels." I kissed her. "See you tonight or tomorrow."

"Yes. Good luck."

Frank started the jeep again, and a great cloud of smoke billowed from the exhaust pipe. I got into the front seat and slammed the door. "All right," I said. Frank engaged the clutch, turned on the lights and started down the driveway. He did not pause at the juncture of the driveway and road; there would be no traffic at this hour, in this cold. The snow plow had not yet been down the road, and the snow was deep and marked only by the grooves of the jeep's earlier passage. The headlights reflected brightly off the snow and illuminated the undersides of the branches of the trees lining the street. The heater fan blew icy air on my legs. The tire chains made a regular thumping sound, and a loose link clattered against the fender. We reached the town limits and drove slowly down the silent black streets. Snow-buried cars were hunched along the curbs. All the street lights had halos. The only moving vehicle we saw was a police car. Frank made a left turn onto one of the side streets.

"I forgot something, too," he said.

"What?"

"My rifle."

"Let me out at the corner."

"Jack, Ralph could easily make it down to Columbine Meadows."

"Sure he could. And he could blow off your head at about five hundred yards. You'd never get the rifle off your back; you'd never even see him. Worse than that, he'd kill me, too, because I was with you."

Frank parked the jeep in front of his house. A light burned yellowly behind the window shades. A shadow appeared behind one window, then vanished, and the porch light was turned on.

"Frank," I said quietly, "you aren't thinking like those macho sheriff's-posse types, are you?"

"Jack, you know me better than that."

"Because if you are, I'm going home."

"Jack, listen—"

"Because it isn't our job to hunt down and kill Ralph Brace. Our job is to go up there and see if we can find those college kids and get them down out of the mountains before they freeze to death or Ralph stumbles onto them. That's all."

Frank turned off the engine, and we were immediately swallowed by the humming silence. "I'm not going up there unarmed," he said. "I don't care to be a mechanical duck in a shooting gallery, like those poor bastards on the chair lift yesterday morning."

"Carrying a rifle is the logical thing to do," I said.

"Well, then?"

"You're being completely rational, Frank."

"Come on," he said.

"Except that Ralph isn't logical or rational. He's crazy. And if he's up there around the Columbine and he sees that one of us is armed . . ."

"Yeah. Mrs. Fielding was armed. Those hitchhikers had pistols in each hand and knives between their teeth.

Those people on the chairs had mortars and grenades and Apollo missiles."

"He didn't hurt the children. He could have."

"That's wonderful, Jack."

"That shows he's still discriminating."

Frank laughed. "Discriminating! Beautiful!"

"It's true."

"Discriminating, huh, Jack?"

"Forget it."

"You're talking crap. Just crap."

"I don't think he would hurt us, Frank. Unless you carry a rifle."

"Jack, listen to me. You're wrong. You're smarter than I am, but you're always wrong about people because you think they're much more complex than they really are. They—we're devious, Jack, but not really complex. Look, forget the psychology. Jack, we *are* what we do. It's that simple; everything else is just a con. Don't look for subtleties of character. Ralph Brace is a bloody murderous son of a bitch, and he'd shoot you or me down as quickly as he would a stranger."

"He didn't hurt the children."

"So what? Damn it, Jack, so what?"

"I don't know," I said. "Forget it."

"What does it mean not to kill children when you have the opportunity?"

"Let's go into the house," I said.

"Look, both you and I were friendly with Ralph. Right? But that was about a year ago—we haven't seen much of him lately. Okay, Ralph used to be our pal. But he wasn't the same man then as he is now."

"Why isn't he?"

"I don't *care* why!"

"Frank, what happened to him?"

"I don't care! All I am trying to tell you is that the guy we drank beer with is not the same guy who's running around the mountains like a werewolf. The character and the action have changed. I'm taking my rifle."

"Okay. And I'll decide whether or not I want to come with you."

"Fine."

"It's just that a lot of people around here seem to regard Ralph Brace as an important big-game trophy."

"Do you think I'm like them, Jack?"

"No."

"Tell me the truth."

"No, Frank, I really don't think you're like them."

"I was about to get mad."

"So was I," I said.

"But, Jack, I don't understand your attitude toward Ralph."

"I just want to keep thinking of him as a man, while everyone else is turning him into a beast."

"No, he became a beast first, and then people began regarding him as one."

"Frank—"

"I'm taking my rifle."

"Frank," I said, "I think you're wrong."

"Jack, I wish you were right."

We got out of the jeep and walked up the snowy walk, mounted the porch steps and entered the house. It was warm inside and smelled of coffee and bacon. Frank went down the narrow hallway leading toward the bedrooms. I sat on the sofa and paged through an issue of *Time* magazine.

Mary Treblene came out of the kitchen, drying her hands on a towel. "Good morning," she said.

"Good morning, Mary."

"Where's Frank?"

"In the bedroom. He forgot something."

"How is Jan?" she asked.

"Fine."

"And the kids?"

"Fiendish. And yours?"

"Billy has a cold. Or the flu, I don't know. Are you happy to be going on vacation?"

"I wish it had started yesterday."

Frank entered the room carrying his 30.06 rifle with the telescopic sight. "You can take the thirty-thirty if you want," he said to me.

"No, thanks."

"Frank, why are you taking a gun?" Mary asked.

"I might get a shot at some coyotes while we're up there," he said.

"Frank?"

I got up and the three of us moved toward the door. Treblene leaned down and kissed his wife lightly on the cheek. "Don't worry about me," he said.

"Frank, be careful."

He moved away and opened the door, allowing a rush of cold air to penetrate the room. "It's okay," he said.

On impulse, I leaned over and kissed her. Her lips were warm and scented with toothpaste. "Don't worry about me," I said.

She smiled briefly. "Frank . . . ?"

We walked down through the snow to the jeep. A few derelict snowflakes drifted through the air.

THREE

All of the buildings along the main street of town were darkened except for George Stanger's sporting goods store; the display windows blazed whitely, colored neons blinked and vibrated, and red neon ducks flapped from left to right about the marquee. The marquee wished everyone a joyful Christmas season. "Headquarters" had been established here, probably because there was not room at the various police stations—state, town and county—for an operation of this size; and because George was providing much of the equipment that would be used during the hunt. And, too, George was a town councilman, and "marshal" of the Wolf County sheriffs posse. The sheriff's posse was composed of store owners and local businessmen and farmers and tradesmen who would much rather have been cowboy-lawmen in the late eighteen hundreds than what they were. They lived very ordinary lives and dreamed of the romantic myths of the old West; they rode their horses in rodeo parades, held quick-draw contests at their clubhouse, raced quarter horses, conducted searches for children who had wandered away from campgrounds. They lived in or near a wealthy, sophisticated community and secretly pretended it was a wild trail town. I knew most of them and liked them. They were good people, but I did not like to see what Ralph Brace had done to them. Their private dream had come alive; their play sheriff's posse had become an actual sheriff's posse; they'd been deputized, and now they tasted adventure, they tasted human blood. They walked differently; they moved and talked more slowly; they challenged you with their eyes. Ralph would probably kill a half dozen of them.

A bell tinkled as we went through the door. It was hot and smoky inside, and Frank's glasses immediately steamed over. He removed his glasses, folded them and slipped them into a pocket.

"I'll see what I can find out," Frank said.

I nodded.

The big store was crowded; there was a low rumble of voices. Smoke coiled and uncoiled through the air like wispy snakes.

At least half of the men were in uniform: policemen from the three agencies, some of my colleagues from the Forest Service, even members of the State Game and Fish Department. The sheriff's posse wore a kind of uniform, too; cowboy boots, Levi's, Stetsons, sheepskin jackets, buckskin finger mittens. They would fill every bed in the hospital with frostbite cases if they did not dress more sensibly before going up onto the mountain. Some members of a snowmobile club were here as well, overweight men in red jumpsuits and rubber Korea boots. A tragedy was well on the way to turning into a farce. The thing was, the only police agency competent to handle the situation, the State Police, was not in charge; the troopers had been called in, but they were subordinate to the county sheriff. The sheriff was a sixty-eight-year-old politician who seemed preoccupied with chasing hippies out of the area. The city police force was made up of local boys who needed a job.

A coffee urn had been set up on the long glass handgun counter. Beside a tall cylinder of paper cups were paper plates, a mound of doughnuts, and bowls containing cream and sugar. Eileen Stanger, George's wife, was standing behind the counter. Weariness had deprived her of some of her almost childish prettiness; she looked like a debauched adolescent now. She appeared tired, separated from all that was happening here. A gun-fighter-electrician said something to her. She smiled gaily, eyes bright, but as soon as the man was gone her smile slowly died, and there was something bitter about the curve of her lips. It had been a convincing smile, too.

I walked over to the counter. "Hello, Eileen."

"Hello, Jack," she said, smiling again.

"Do you mind if I have some coffee?"

"Of course not, silly. That's what it's here for, to drink."

I took one of the paper cups, turned the little silver lever on the urn, and watched the stream of black coffee twist down into my cup. I added a little sugar and cream. Beneath the glass counter top I could see dozens of ugly blue-black pistols and revolvers.

"You forgot to shave, Jack."

"I may grow a beard," I said.

"Be careful, or the town may accidentally sweep you out along with the hippies."

"I know. Hippies make the condominiums look cheap. Are you an elitist, Eileen?"

"You bet."

I sipped the coffee. "What are your qualifications to be an elitist?"

She smiled.

"Seriously, I would like to know. I have nothing against elitists; I just wonder how one qualifies. Are you elected by secret ballot by established elitists? Or do you experience an irresistible inner calling?"

She smiled again. "Jack Marty, our very own village iconoclast, asking his Socratic-type questions."

"Don't make me sound cute or I'll blow up a power station."

"But you are cute, Jack."

"Do you want to hear a funny Polish joke, Eileen?" Her maiden name was Pokorski.

"No," she said.

"It's really hilarious, Eileen."

"Never mind," she said, and she began to laugh prematurely at the joke she refused to hear.

"You're an angel out of heaven, Eileen. Stay away from me; I'll only hurt you."

"Poor Jan."

"Careful with that 'poor Jan' stuff or she'll come up here and pop you once or twice."

"Jack," she said, "you're clever and all that, but you have no character."

I laughed, though I was not certain she was kidding.

"Listen, is it true? I heard that Mr. Brooks asked you to resign from the Forest Service."

"That was last week. He likes me this week."

"What was it about?"

"I told him he was the lackey of the lumber and cattle and ski resort interests."

"But that isn't true!"

"Of course it's true."

"And did you hit him?"

"No, but I shoved him a little."

"Jack, you're never going to rise in the Forest Service."

"That is a perceptive observation."

"Jack, seriously, how long do you think you can go on being so irresponsible?"

"Much longer than you can go on being so responsible, Eileen." I finished my coffee and started away from the counter.

"Jack, aren't you going to tell me the joke?"

"Not until I perfect the accent."

I wandered away from the gun counter. There was a lot of movement and noise in the store, but no one seemed to be doing anything. A vast amount of equipment was spread out over the floor: snow vehicles, skis and poles, snowshoes, down clothing, lightweight radio equipment, cartons of dehydrated food, rifles and ammunition, binoculars, coils of rope . . . It looked as if preparations were being made for a three-month expedition. War is expensive.

I spent some time looking over the new ski equipment. There was a pair of Rossignol slalom skis that I would have liked to own, but since they cost nearly $250, I decided my old skis would do nicely for another year.

There were a dozen strangers wandering around the room; journalists, I guessed. Newspaper and television journalists had started arriving in town a few hours after the killings; they had made the last hop from Denver and Salt Lake City in four-wheel-drive vehicles, State Highway Department snow plows and trucks; and one character, from the CBS affiliate in Denver, had skied over Elk Creek Pass when his car had stalled. During the worst part of the storm, when even ambulances did not attempt to leave the area, the journalists flocked in like a new, winter-adapted migratory species—one instant there were none, the next instant the sky had become dark and you were deafened by the thunderclap of their wings. I had talked to a few of them; I liked them, but I wished they wouldn't talk as if a sniper on the rampage were a semi-miraculous piece of personal good fortune. It might be good for their careers, better than the Texas Tower Sniper and the New Orleans Sniper, but it was embarrassing to hear them say so. They were all very ambitious. I preferred the old type of journalist: shabby, either drunk or hungover, cynical. These new men reminded me of accountants or FBI agents. I feared that they had all been cloned by the University of Missouri Journalism School.

I eavesdropped on a few of the sheriff's-posse types: they were discussing things like muzzle velocity and grains and windage and feet-per-second, and how it was best to use something with real knockdown power when you were going after an armed man. A man named Tom Horne said he had been deer hunting two years earlier and some dumb son of a bitch had been glassing the country with the telescopic sight on his rifle: "He looked at me through his 'scope, just looking, but I didn't know that, and I snapped off a couple of shots. I buzzed his ears. He'll never look at another man down the barrel of his rifle." The others laughed and hurried to tell similar stories.

It was depressing. I hoped they were not so stupid as they sounded. If they were going up on the mountain tomorrow with the heroic notion of playing point man, Ralph Brace would kill them. They used euphemisms like "greased" and "chopped," when the right word was "killed." Maybe one or more of them would be greased before sunset. If so, the NRA might send his wife and kids a plaque and a year's free subscription to the magazine.

Tom Horne noticed me. "Jack," he said, "have you got a piece?" He was wearing a holstered .357 magnum revolver slung gunfighter style around his waist. Tom was a member of the clique within the clique, the men who talked about guerrilla warfare against Russians after the nuclear catastrophe.

"What is a 'piece,' Tom?" I knew what a piece was; it just seemed to me that a man ought to call a gun a gun.

He smiled. "That's a rifle, Jack, or a pistol."

"No, I'm not a hostile in this war."

"What do the neutrals do?"

"We roll bandages and sell poppies."

"Jack, I hope you told Ralph Brace you're a neutral."

"He'll know by the red cross on my back."

"Or maybe by the yellow on your back," Tom Horne said, and the others laughed with him.

"Easy, Tom," I said. "Don't get bold just because you're wearing your balls in a holster today."

"I was just kidding, Jack," he said, grinning at me. The others were grinning, too.

"Well, okay. I was only kidding when I made you a cuckold."

They were all laughing when I walked away. Happy fellows.

I was looking for Frank when I felt a touch on my shoulder. I turned.

"Hello, Jack."

It was Ray Plessing, a reporter for the local daily newspaper and a stringer for the Associated Press.

"Hi, Ray," I said. "Newshawking, are you?"

"I'm gathering quotes," he said. "Do you have a quote for me?"

"Why, yes, I do."

He removed a notebook and pencil from his breast pocket. "Speak slowly," he said. "I have to mentally translate the English into Sanskrit."

"Let them eat cake," I said.

He scribbled in his notebook. "That's a beauty."

"Do you want another quote, Ray?"

"Certainly, if it's of equal caliber."

"Frankly, Scarlett, I don't give a damn."

"That's wonderful. One more, Jack, please."

"That depends, sir, upon whether I embrace your principles or your mistress."

"I'm sated," he said, putting away his notebook.

"Is this business any kind of break for you, Ray?"

"No. The Denver AP bureau chief arrived in town yesterday. He didn't trust me with this story."

"That's too bad."

"I'm just gathering facts and quotes. The AP man will write the major stories. I may get to do a short feature article, though."

"Do you want another quote?"

"Sure."

"A bird in the hand is worth two in the bush."

"The quality is falling off. Jack, listen, has he talked to you yet? I sicked him onto you."

"You sicked who onto me?"

"The AP man, Harry Ormond. That's him brooding over there with his back to the wall, beneath the antelope head. I told him that Ralph worked for you and that you were pretty good friends, and that you know this country, and he said he was going to talk to you."

"No, he hasn't approached me."

"He's a pretty good guy, Jack. Why don't we walk over there, and I'll introduce you to him."

"Curious," I said. "I have the feeling I've been surrounded by a single person."

Ray grinned. "Come on," he said.

"Why can't I just talk to you?"

"Because I'm just a stringer, a flunkey in the great scheme of things."

"Will it help you any if I talk to him?"

"It won't hurt me, Jack."

"Okay."

Harry Ormond was a tall, alert-looking man of about forty. He had salt-and-pepper hair, a crooked nose, and bright, oddly fierce-looking eyes. I didn't like his eyes until it occurred to me that he probably wore contact lenses. He was courteous in a relaxed way, soft-voiced, ironically self-deprecating.

Ray Plessing wandered off in search of quotes.

"Ray wants a job with your outfit," I said.

"I know."

"Are you going to give him one?"

"Maybe in a year or two." Ormond removed a topographical map from the pocket of his overcoat, unfolded it and spread it against the wall.

"Can you read those things?" I asked.

"Not very well, and I badly need orienting."

"Well, look, there is a big bas-relief map of the district over at the Forest Service office. It's formed to scale, and you'll be able to clearly understand the terrain."

"Will you take me over there?"

"Sure. But I can't stay long."

"I'd appreciate any time you can spend with me," Ormond said.

"Ray Plessing is an enterprising kid," I said. "He might be ready for a job with your office sooner than you think."

Ormond nodded and refolded his map. "I'll see how he does during the next few days."

FOUR

The cold again surprised me: there was no way to prepare your mind and body for the light, insinuating touch of that cold. We started walking through the snow.

"You were a friend of Ralph Brace?" Ormond asked.

"Yes."

"You were his only friend, I guess."

"No, he had friends."

"Everyone I've talked to has denied being his friend."

"Does that surprise you?"

"Do you still consider him a friend?"

"Oddly enough, yes. But within a few days I should be able to regard him as an acquaintance."

Harry Ormond laughed. "How long will it take for him to become a stranger?"

"Ask his acquaintances. They're one step ahead of me."

The Forest Service building was located on a side street three blocks from the sporting goods store. I unlocked the door, opened it, flipped all the light switches and turned up the thermostat.

There was a six-by-six-foot table in the center of the visitors' room which contained a bas-relief map of the entire Forest Service district. It had been molded out of papier-mâché to scale and then painted to look like the terrain it represented; blue for lakes and streams; green for the forested mountains, with the land above timberline a grayish brown; white for the ski trails; dotted brown lines for footpaths; the highways black with a white center line. The Wolf Mountain Wilderness Area was enclosed by a thin red line, indicating that no motorized transport of any kind—airplane, motorcycle, four-wheel-drive vehicle, snowmobile—was permitted to enter.

"Okay," I said. "This crosshatching here in the valley is the town, of course. Ralph had a room on the eastern edge. I suppose you've been to the roominghouse?"

"I was there yesterday."

"Right. Now, Ralph murdered his landlady, Mrs. Fielding, and then loaded his jeep with part of his belongings. He drove north out of town on the main highway. Right about here is where he killed the two hitchhikers. I don't know whether he shot them while passing, or stopped."

"The cops say the hitchhikers were killed from close range."

"Then he stopped his car and shot them when they started to get in."

"A sweet guy."

"He continued down the highway and turned west here, onto a jeep road which isn't shown on this map.

Actually, you can hardly call it a road—it's just a swath cut through the trees and brush so that we can get heavy equipment up into that country in case of a fire. It can also serve as a firebreak."

"He didn't get very far."

"No, just a few hundred yards. I'm surprised he made it as far as he did; the road isn't maintained during the winter. He knew he'd get stuck. Now, he got out of the jeep, gathered all of his gear—food, sleeping bag, tent, rucksack, weapons, skis and poles—and started climbing. Did you go out there when they found the jeep?"

"Yes."

"Did you see his tracks?"

"They'd been pretty well covered with new snow by the time I arrived."

"Over here, you see, is the northernmost ski trail on the mountain. It's serviced by a double chair. Ralph climbed upward and toward the southwest, intersecting the trail just about here. Are you a skier?"

Ormond shook his head.

"Ralph picked his shot. Forgive the pun. Below his position, the chair rises up over a steep hill and then crosses a kind of gully to the top of another hill. The gully is about two hundred feet wide and a hundred feet deep below the chair cable."

"There was no place for them to go," Ormond said.

"Except down. As you know, some of the skiers did jump out of the chairs during the shooting."

"The crafty son of a bitch."

"Ralph was in the forested section alongside the trail, roughly one hundred and twenty-five feet away from the chairs, as the bullet flies. Remember that the chairs were also one hundred feet above him. Okay, so picture Ralph with a comfortable shooting position and chairs popping into view over the lower hill and then moving left to right across his field of vision."

"Like a shooting gallery."

"Exactly."

"What is this dot up here?"

"The upper lift terminal."

"Someone made it through on a chair and warned the lift operator, and he turned off the power."

"Yes, and left half a dozen chairs hanging over the gully. But they were mostly kids going up to join ski school, and Ralph didn't shoot them. He shot their instructors, but he didn't hit any children."

"A generous fellow. But some of the kids jumped."

"Right, and earlier some adults had jumped, too. So what was the toll?—thirteen killed by rifle fire, including Mrs. Fielding and the two hitchhikers; three wounded; and seven hurt by jumping. Those who jumped were lucky; the deepness of the snow absorbed much of the impact."

"Fourteen killed," Ormond said. "One of the wounded died two hours ago. And two of the jumpers are listed in critical condition."

"This isn't the end of it," I said. "Ralph will kill some more before they finally get him. Especially with all these deer hunters wandering around up on the mountain."

"I suppose you're right."

"You can bet I'm right. This isn't some urban sniper pinned down in a single building. That's bad enough. But Ralph is young, strong, a competent outdoorsman; and he knows this country well. He can play Vietcong up there and maybe last for a week."

"I've heard they're going to call in some National Guard helicopters and crews."

"I wouldn't want to be a pilot."

"Where do you suppose Brace is at this moment?"

"In the Summit House, frying hamburgers and drinking beer."

"The sheriff is talking about going up in the cable car this morning."

"The sheriff is prematurely senile. I can promise you that the cable car is not working. Ralph has seen to that. The sheriff will have to climb on skis or snowshoes, like everyone else."

"So you see this as a difficult situation."

I laughed.

"Ray Plessing told me you're going up to find some college kids. Where are they?"

"God only knows. We hope they're at this dot—that's the Columbine Cabin."

"Go on."

"They took the cable car up to the Summit House yesterday morning, ascended to this high ridge, skied the ridge for several miles to this col, you see, and then skied off the col into the upper meadows. The storm started about an hour after they left the Summit House.

If they managed to locate the cabin in all the snow and cloud, good; we'll find them and bring them down. If they missed the cabin . . ." I shrugged.

"What if Brace goes down there?"

"I don't believe he will. This is his last stand. He's committing suicide, and he wants to take a lot of company with him. No, I think he'll stay up on the mountain, or even come back down into town, where there'll be plenty of characters to escort him to hell."

"How are you going to reach this cabin?"

"We'll circle around to the south and enter through this narrow valley."

"How did you learn the college kids were going there?"

"That's the itinerary they left with the Ski Patrol. All wilderness skiers have to register with either the Ski Patrol or the Forest Service."

"What kind of guy is Ralph Brace?" Ormond asked.

"Christ. There's a question."

He smiled. "Like, what kind of guy was Lee Harvey Oswald?"

"No, not at all, not at all like that. Ralph was, is—I *liked* Ralph. He doesn't fit your usual assassin profile. I mean, he wasn't one of those sullen, sneaky, megalomaniacal punks."

"What *was* he, then?"

"Listen, Ormond, would you like a drink?"

"Do you have something with you?"

"No, but an employee here, Ruth Schmidt, has a drawer full of booze. She decants it into medicine bottles at home and drinks it here during the days, under the theory, no doubt, that it's better to be considered a hypochondriac than a lush. She's just a year away from retirement, and so no one says anything. We pretend it really is medicine unless we care to steal a drink."

"Well, I could use a little cough syrup."

"Cough syrup is bourbon."

"Pepto-Bismol?"

"Vodka with a lot of grenadine."

He laughed. "Is this on the level?"

"Ruth is a nice woman. Muddled, but nice."

"What about brandy?"

"A strong emetic in an eight-ounce brown bottle."

"Well, let's have an emetic."

"Right. I can brew some coffee if you'd like."

"I prefer my emetics straight."

"Good, you're a man after my own colon."

We entered the office section, and I went through the bottles in Ruth's desk until I found a nearly full bottle of Remy Martin emetic. I got a couple of paper cups from the dispenser at the water cooler and filled them halfway with cognac.

Ormond facetiously swirled the cognac in his paper cup, sniffed it, tasted. "Hey," he said, "this is decent stuff."

"Look, Ormond, we don't hire just any kind of drunk here. You'll find your degenerate Thunderbird winos working for the National Park Service."

"What kind of guy was Ralph Brace?"

"I'm sure you've heard most of his history."

"Everyone I've talked to so far has said that he'd always known Ralph was a dangerous psychopath."

"Hindsight," I said. "They look at the world out of their rectums. They can't see anything until just before it vanishes over the horizon."

"Can I quote you?"

"Sure. My name is Informed Local Source. Ormond, what can I tell you that you haven't already heard?"

"How long did you know him?"

"Four years."

"You were friends that long?"

"No. I didn't know him well the first year he was in town, and I haven't seen much of him during the last year."

"Why haven't you seen much of him during the last year?"

I shrugged. "He's stayed to himself."

"Did you ever see him with other people?"

"Rarely."

"He withdrew, then; he became solitary?"

"Yes, that's right."

"When you saw him, was he friendly to you?"

"He wasn't *un*friendly. He was a little cool, maybe—distant."

"What was he like during the two years when you were friends?"

"Oh, cheerful, a damned hard worker when he worked, a little shy sometimes, good company—you looked for him at the end of the work day. A little reckless."

"What do you know about his past, before he moved here?"

"Well, he's from Denver. His family still lives there."

"His mother and stepfather arrived here last night," Ormond said.

"Really? Have you met them?"

"She held a press conference."

"What are they like?"

"She's a tragic figure."

"Come on."

"She's horrible—a dreary martyr, as sentimental as a third-grader's valentine, so maudlin it makes you a little sick. She loves the publicity. She refers to herself in the third person. 'Ralph's mother.' You know? 'Ralph's mother will stand behind her only son.' That kind of thing, and she uses the word 'love' a lot, like most people who can't feel anything. She pretends to feel deeply; she tries to imitate the real thing, but of course it comes out a parody."

"Ralph's stepfather?"

"He seems concerned only with making everyone understand that Ralph is not his blood son. He's a kind of weedy character, and his eyes seem to focus about six inches in front of your own eyes."

"What happened to Ralph's real father?"

"He vanished twenty years ago."

"Well . . ."

"What do you know about Ralph's youth?"

"I understand he was a good high school athlete, All-State in both football and basketball, a good skier.

He was a top student, too, until his senior year, when I guess he became something of a hell-raiser. But I figured that any high school boy who isn't a little wild shouldn't be trusted—he might grow up to be a state senator."

"Ralph has a sheet in Denver."

"So I've heard. Drunk and disorderly, simple assault, automobile theft—joyriding, he said. He stayed out of jail."

"He was charged with rape, too, along with a couple other guys."

"I hadn't heard about that."

"They were acquitted. And he nearly killed a guy in Jackson, Wyoming, when he was twenty-one. Stabbed him during a bar quarrel."

"I didn't know about that."

"Ralph left town fast."

"Well, Christ."

"Another rape complaint was filed in this town eighteen months ago, but the girl withdrew the complaint after two days—she wanted to avoid the embarrassment of a trial."

"I heard something about that, but I just figured some girl had said no *after* the consummation."

"Jack, do you remember when the body of a fifteen-year-old runaway girl was found here last winter? Naked, terribly mutilated?"

"No, Ralph didn't do that."

"No one thought so at the time, but the State Police now think he was responsible."

"That's a damned good way to close the books on an unsolved murder," I said.

"It's also an entirely natural assumption. I believe Ralph Brace did it. The cops are certain he did. Look at it: this character has a long history of violence, including rape. And now murder. Many murders."

"But I knew Ralph. I would have sensed *something.*"

"You probably should have, Jack, but you didn't. Now keep going."

"I'm learning more about him than you are."

"I don't want facts from you. I want your subjective appraisal of the man, how you saw him."

"I'm beginning to doubt that I knew him."

"You didn't, really. Incidentally, did Ralph tell you he was All-State in football and basketball?"

"Yes."

"He lied. He didn't play either sport, and he dropped out of high school when he was sixteen."

"Well. What can I say?"

"He lied about a lot of things to you and everyone else. He has a history of lying that goes back to grammar school. When he was in the eighth grade, and again when he was a freshman, he was referred to the school district's psychiatrist. I read the reports. Ralph was adjudged to be a sociopathic personality."

"A psychopath," I said.

"That's what they used to be called."

"Christ, I should have sensed something."

"Don't feel too bad. Sociopaths are often highly intelligent and very charming. And they're not all recognized as criminals, either. Hitler and Stalin were sociopaths—that's easy. But so are a lot of others, people in the arts, business, politics, everywhere. They con a lot of people. It's almost an attribute of the sociopath—their ability to con."

"Well, apparently I was conned."

"It was stupid of me to interrupt this way. I've probably altered your perceptions of Ralph Brace. But try to honestly tell me how you saw him, before all of this happened."

"I saw him as intelligent, though not well educated."

"Yes."

"Open and friendly—charming."

Ormond smiled. "Yes."

"Sometimes too open, too charming—he'd sometimes attract people whom I disliked."

"Creepy types? That is, losers, the lost?"

"Sometimes, yes."

"Victims," Ormond said. "Was he ever incoherent?"

"No, I don't think I could say that he was."

"Even when he was drunk?"

"No more than anyone else who's had too much to drink."

"No?"

"In fact, he was less rambling and disconnected than most men who are drunk."

"Did he drink to excess often?"

"Yes."

"Did he use drugs?"

"I don't know."

"He never mentioned drugs to you?"

"No."

"He knew you weren't a user. When he was in the company of users, he talked about drugs, and he sold drugs, too. He was whatever he believed his companions wanted him to be. Listen, wasn't there anything distinctive about him when he'd had too much to drink?"

"I don't know. It's been awhile, and as I told you, I didn't see Ralph much during the last year."

"Would you say that he was a manipulative type of man?"

"Now I would, yes. But I wouldn't have thought so then. I didn't think so."

"Was he contemptuous?"

"Sometimes, yes."

"Like he knew something no one else in the world knew?"

"Well, yes . . . I think that's true."

"Did you ever have a feeling of danger when he got into these manipulative, contemptuous moods?"

"No."

"Did he use people?"

"I can see that he did, now, sure."

"Did he use you, Jack?"

"Yes. I never had the feeling of being used, but now, looking back, I can see that I was."

"How?"

"How else? Money, time, effort."

"Was he generous with money?"

"Yes, when he had it."

"Was he often broke?"

"Off and on. When he had money he spent it. He used to buy Jan—my wife—gifts."

"Did your wife like Ralph?"

"No."

"The wives of your other friends?"

"No."

"Did women in general like him?"

"Some types."

"What kind of women were attracted to him?"

"Oh, I don't know. Young hippie girls, mystics, bead-stringers, and some older women."

"Troubled people?"

"Okay."

"Would you say that Ralph Brace disliked women?"

I thought about that. "Yes, but he wasn't a homosexual."

"Misogyny and homosexuality aren't synonymous. Was he promiscuous?"

"Yes, but I can hardly fault him for that. If I were single, I'd be promiscuous, too."

"Wouldn't we all? Did men like him?"

"Some. Others didn't."

"How did you become his friend?"

"That's a dumb question, Ormond."

"No, it isn't. Think about it."

I thought about it. "We worked together."

"Propinquity breeds familiarity," Ormond said. "Do you believe that you would have become Ralph's friend if you hadn't worked with him?"

"No," I said. "But I wouldn't have invented myself if my parents hadn't taken the same bus one day. I wouldn't have met my wife if she hadn't broken her leg skiing. I wouldn't have met my son if I hadn't gotten heated up at a Sophia Loren movie. My daughter was the product of lust, too, but I don't recall the exact inspiration. It might have been Jan herself. It's true; Ralph and I would not have become friendly if we hadn't worked together."

"Don't get mad," Ormond said.

"I'm not getting mad. It's just that you keep trying to squeeze Ralph into your preconceived profile. He is all that you say he is, okay, but he was more, too. He was—is still, perhaps—three-dimensional, and you've only apprehended one dimension. And you've flattened me while flattening him."

"Earlier, you said that he was a little reckless."

"He was."

"Can you tell me about it?"

"We worked together on avalanche control."

"Avalanche control?"

"Do you want some more emetic?"

"No, thanks."

"I'll have a little more. Keep Ruth from temptation." I poured some cognac into my paper cup. "Don't you take notes?" I asked him.

"Notes might get in the way of fantasy. What is this about avalanche control?"

"You'll need a little background, I suppose. Eight years ago the Forest Service sent me to an avalanche school in Alta, Utah. They were ahead of us in Utah, then. They probably still are. Anyway, it was a three-week cram course, practical work in the mountains in the mornings and classroom study during the afternoons. It was a fairly new thing for the Forest Service to get into. Bureaucratic infiltration—leave an opening and the paper shufflers will fill it. No, wait, that isn't fair. There was a real need for some agency to assume responsibility for avalanche control, and since a large part of Colorado, a large part of all the Western states, is public land administered by the Forest Service, it was natural enough—listen, Ormond, if this is boring you . . ."

"I'm yawning because I've had three hours' sleep in the last forty-eight hours. Sorry. It has nothing to do with your dry, pedantic, monotonal delivery."

"Okay. There have always been avalanches in the mountains, of course, but only in recent years have they become a big problem. Many of the new roads, ski areas, resort communities and so forth occupy potentially dangerous sites. Five skiers have been killed in avalanches so far this year, and spring is a long way off. Five or six motorists have been killed in slides. Ormond?"

"I'm listening, Jack."

"After my training in Utah I was assigned to work here, at this ski area. Two members of the Ski Patrol, hired by the corporation, were placed under my authority. Ralph Brace was one of them. Our task, basically, was to prevent the embarrassment and bad publicity resulting from having tourists killed by avalanches while vacationing here. We usually succeeded. When we failed, the corporation and the Forest Service would announce that the unfortunate skier was killed while skiing on a closed trail."

"They lied?"

"Yes."

"They covered up?"

"Yes, it was a cover-up, literally and metaphorically. Think of the lawsuits if they didn't lie."

"Go on."

"And sometimes I was loaned out to the State Highway Department, before the department trained one of their own men."

"Jack, you said Ralph Brace was reckless."

"Yes, but so was the other guy, Terry Braden. So was I until I got buried one morning."

"Maybe I will have a little more cognac."

I got the bottle and poured some into his cup.

"What was your job?" he asked.

"We could reach most of the important ski trails with the howitzer, but there are remote trails and bowls and corniced ridges in the back country. After a big storm, or in the spring when the warmth and winds made snow conditions especially dangerous, we'd stuff our rucksacks full of explosives and go out and make booms. If a slope was ready to avalanche, a couple cans of explosives would shake it loose, and generally it would then be safe for skiing, although you have to make sure there aren't any secondary avalanches ready to slide. I liked the work. We had some really fine virgin powder skiing, and we got to play with firecrackers, too."

"Ralph was wild, though?"

"Yeah, he was a little crazy at times, but he was just a kid. He's still just a kid, twenty-five or twenty-six. Ralph excelled at blowing cornices. Do you know what a cornice is?"

"Sure. I think so."

"The winds blow all winter over these ridges and form a wave of snow that's twenty, thirty feet high. They look like a big ocean wave that's just on the verge of breaking. Ralph would stand on the high point of a ridge and activate a few cans of the explosive. They came in canisters, about the size of a pint beer can. The canisters had different fuse times and were color-coded so we'd know which was which. For example, the red can had a ten-second fuse; the green, eight seconds; the black, six. Well, Ralph might activate three cans, a red, a green, and a black, and then ski like hell down the ridge, just below the potential fracture line of the cornice. Jesus! A live bomb in each hand and one beneath his armpit. Have you got the picture, Ormond? All right, he's flying down the ridge and he tosses the black can over the lip of the cornice. Bang! A huge geyser of snow and a concussion you can feel in your belly fifty yards away, but by that time Ralph is farther down the ridge, and it's time for the green can. Bang! Same thing, and then the red can."

"Time is up," Ormond said.

"Just about. The red can, and Ralph has vanished in this enormous sparkling cloud of snowflakes. Terry Braden and I would look down the ridge, and the cornice is mostly gone, snow is settling everywhere, maybe the slab of snow beneath the cornice has broken loose and a hundred tons of snow blocks are tumbling down the mountain. Utter chaos. Later, when we'd catch up with Ralph, he would be grinning from ear to ear. He loved it. Of course, all he'd have had to do was fall or be a little slow in getting rid of a canister, and it would have been all over for him."

"Too bad something like that never happened."

"Yeah, it is, isn't it?"

"Ralph worked for the Ski Corporation at that time?"

"During the winters. In the summers he worked for the Forest Service as a seasonal employee. Cutting trails, building shelters—donkey work."

"You did like him, didn't you, Jack?"

I nodded.

"You saw him three-dimensionally."

"No," I said. "Two, just two. I never saw this final dimension."

"What else can you tell me about him?"

"Nothing, now," I said, rising from my chair. "Frank and I have to get started."

I turned off the lights and locked the door behind us. It was dark, cold, silent—the long primal night. We walked down the snowy side streets. Street lights ignited the snow, made it blaze whitely.

"I'm confused as hell," I said.

"Sure."

"Ralph didn't hurt the children."

"Jack, there's no law that says that sociopaths can't be sentimental. Maybe they're more sentimental than other people. On the night of the La Bianca murders,

Charlie Manson rejected one house because he saw photographs of children inside—he didn't think his gang should kill children at that time, you see. Don't get sidetracked by Ralph's inconsistencies. We're all inconsistent, and psychotics more than anyone."

We walked the rest of the way in silence and paused outside the sporting goods store.

"I'm going to try to sleep for a couple of hours," Ormond said. "Thanks for your help."

We shook hands.

"You told me a hell of a lot more than I told you," I said.

"I learned something," he said. "More than you might think. Listen, when you get down out of the mountains, call me, will you? I'm at the Holiday Inn, room forty-two."

"Sure, I'll call."

"Bye, Jack."

"Take it easy," I said.

FIVE

Frank was leaning against the gun counter when I entered the store. He straightened. "Where the hell have you been?"

"Doing some PR work. Let's go."

"Jack, things are all fouled up."

"What do you mean?"

"I have orders from the sheriff that we're not to go up into the mountains without an armed escort."

"What?"

"That's right."

"What kind of armed escort?"

"I don't know. Sheriff's-posse types, I guess."

"What's going on, Frank?"

"Guess."

"Frank . . ."

"Some kind of quasi-martial law, I think, except the sheriff is in charge."

"Frank, you know and I know that the sheriff doesn't know his own name until George Stanger reminds him. What is this? We're Forest Service employees; we're going up into land administered by the Forest Service, on valid Forest Service business."

"Tell the sheriff."

"Have you talked to Brooks?"

"Yeah."

"Well?"

"You know Brooks, Jack."

"What did he say?"

"He said that we're to cooperate with law enforcement officials."

"Yeah?"

"Brooks doesn't have any guts, Jack."

"I know. He may be in charge of the entire Forest Service someday. Look, Frank, this is too much. I feel like chucking the whole thing."

"I know."

"I mean, all we want to do is help some kids who've had bad luck."

"Yeah, I know."

"Have you talked to Stanger?"

"No."

"This is ridiculous. Frank, they're screwing up my sense of reality again."

He grinned.

"It's irrational."

"At least."

"I'm not kidding now—everyone seems to act as if error were the highest virtue. Have you talked to the state cops?"

"The state cops are piqued-off and helpless."

"My God, do you mean that Sheriff Senile Paresis is in charge of this whole business?"

"Yes, until the governor sends in the National Guard."

"Where is Stanger?"

"Over there, in the corner with his irregulars."

"Aw, Frank," I said.

He grinned.

"I am a respecter of law and of lawfully designated authority."

"Me, too."

"What do you think George will say?"

"George will say no."

"Do you want to try him?"

"Why not?"

"We have nothing to lose."

"Except a little self-respect."

"Frank, I don't know—there is some comedy in the situation. Stupidity is funny if you can view it from the correct angle. But they're making me lose my sense of reality. All of these people are qualified to serve in the U.S. Congress. The sheriff could be President."

"Let's confront the scoundrels."

Frank and I approached the group: George Stanger, Tom Horne, Chuck Hughes, Lew Griffin, Art Krause, some others.

George Stanger was a big, barrel-chested man with squinty eyes and thinning blond hair and that waxy translucent complexion that reveals every hair and capillary beneath the surface of the skin. George had once been a heavy drinker, and his nose and cheeks were florid with the mazes of broken blood vessels. He had played two seasons of professional football in the fifties, and he liked to use his size—he was about six foot five and weighed 250 pounds—to intimidate other men; he stood very close, looking down, leaning, not touching you, but making you aware of his size and strength. He was devoted to his wife and two children; was generous and almost fanatically loyal to those whom he considered his friends; had a rough, ribald wit and a laugh that sounded as if it had been struck on a pipe organ. Certain kinds of men were drawn to him, weak men mostly, and they often humiliated themselves and each other trying to gain his good opinion. They admired and feared him. But George was far more intelligent and sensitive than he liked to appear, certainly more so than those men gathered around him like pilot fish; but he seemed ashamed of the gentle side of his nature. We got along well enough, though we were wary of each other; I did not buy his hail-fellow-well-met act, his sometimes paranoid machismo; and he regarded me as insultingly aloof.

"Frank," I said, "what do you think—will they hurt us?"

"I don't know," Frank said. "They're an awesome crowd. Enough firepower here to take Stalingrad."

George Stanger grinned at us. "Well," he said, "if it isn't Mr. Interlocutor and Mr. Bones."

"Hello, George," Frank said.

"Hi, Bones. Hello, Mr. Interlocutor. Did the finance company repossess your razor, Mr. Interlocutor?"

"If God had wanted men to shave," I said, "He would not have given us hair."

"Well, He started taking mine away ten years ago."

"A sign of His displeasure," I said. "Now, George, what is this crap about we can't go up into the mountains without taking along some of your Sunday cowboys?"

"Listen to him," Tom Horne said.

"Shut up, Tom. Jack, that isn't my idea, it's the sheriff's."

"The sheriff hasn't had an idea in thirty years. Don't blow any smoke in my ear, George. Who are you thinking of sending with us?"

"Tom, here, Hughes, Wilcox, Lilith, Krause."

"What do you think, Frank?" I asked.

"I think they could maybe stay with us for a hundred yards."

"Screw you guys," Tom Horne said.

"No, George," I said. "Just because a man goes deer hunting for a week in October doesn't necessarily mean he's an outdoorsman. We'll be going into the high country, close to thirteen thousand feet, and the snow will be chest-deep. It's going to be thirty-five, forty below zero up there. Use your head—you haven't got anyone who's good enough on skis or snowshoes to stay with us."

"You'll all use snowmobiles," George said.

I stared at him. "Frank," I said, "what do you think?"

"Snowmobiles? The trail won't take snowmobiles."

"Cut out the crap," Stanger said. "Either you go with an armed escort or you don't go at all."

"Frank is taking a rifle," I said.

"Bones couldn't hit the wall of a house if he was locked inside."

"I'd have a fifty-fifty chance!" Frank said.

"Clown, you guys. But the sheriff has said that *no one* can go up into the hills without protection. And that's it."

"What if we go anyway?" Frank asked.

"You'll be arrested, arraigned, and heavily fined."

"Judge," I said, "Frank and I know that country. I work up there two or three days a week during the winter. Now, if Frank and I don't go up and get those kids, who's going to?"

"Maybe we will."

"They will, Frank."

"With their machines."

"I'm getting pretty tired of these guys," Tom Horne said.

"George, shut Horne up," Frank said. "Or I'll do it myself."

"Try it," Horne said.

"Look, Bones—"

"Don't call me Bones anymore, George."

"Frank—for God's sake, Frank, there's a maniac running around loose in these mountains—he's killing people—and if you two won't accept the sheriff's conditions, then we'll find men who will."

"Who? Horne, Wilcox, Krause?"

"Sure. Plus there's a mountain rescue group coming in from Boulder, and another from Denver. Now okay, I appreciate that you and Jack are skilled skiers and mountaineers and all, but there are others around who are just as good—maybe better. And younger, too. I think you guys are too old for this job, anyway."

"We're not too old to drink Irish coffee," Frank said. "I've got a jug of Bushmills at home."

"Let's go to my place," I said.

"Okay, we'll stop at the house and pick up the wife and the Bushmills and enjoy this mean winter day."

Stanger smiled. "Now *you're* blowing smoke in *my* ear."

"George, what are *you* going to do?" I asked.

"I'm going after Ralph Brace."

"Good hunting," I said.

"Bon appétit," Frank said.

"George," I said, "listen—screw it. I haven't got the time or the energy to deal with all this bureaucratic bullshit. Send your lickspittles into the mountains, and then send the strong young mountaineers to rescue the lickspittles. I don't care. It's on your head."

Stanger smiled. "Write an outraged letter to the newspaper."

"Let's go," Frank said to me.

"Somehow," Stanger said, "I just don't believe you two intend to go home."

"Come on down and have some Irish coffee," I said.

"I'm too busy."

"Phone us."

"Jack, I understand that your job with the Forest Service isn't too secure these days. It could become even less secure."

"George, don't threaten me."

"Call it advice," he said.

"Well, I have some advice for you, too."

Smiling. "What is it?"

"Come on," Frank said, taking my arm.

"Toughen up before you threaten me again. You're big, George, but you're fat and soft."

"How soft, Jack? Show me."

"Come on, for Christ's sake," Frank said.

We turned and crossed the store and stepped outside.

SIX

We drove south on the main street until there were fewer and fewer buildings, and then the street widened into a highway. The snowdrifts alongside the road were nearly as high as the jeep, and they glowed brightly in the headlights; it was like going down a well-lit tunnel. The road snaked through the low hills in big coils, running parallel to the river. On the curves the headlights shot beyond the road and illuminated the snowy cottonwoods and aspens that grew alongside the river. Once we saw the amber glow of an animal's eyes.

The tire chains clattered and thumped. The heater fan blasted my legs with cold air.

"I knew this was going to be a hard winter," Frank said.

"How did you know that?"

"Oh, we Indians know."

Frank liked to draw attention to his one-eighth Indian ancestry. He had never mentioned it until Indians became fashionable.

"How do you Indians know, Frank?"

"By the size of the white men's woodpiles."

"How do the little birdies know, Frank?"

"I'm not sure. The *Farmer's Almanac?*"

"How do the little furry creatures of the woodlands and marshes know, Frank?"

"Know what?"

"Know that there's going to be an earthquake."

"I wonder," he said.

"Explain the miracle of a spider spinning his web."

"That's a tough one, Jack."

"Does the squishy caterpillar know that he will someday become a beautiful butterfly?"

"Gosh. The mysteries of nature."

"Don't ever forget it."

"I'm glad we had this little talk, Jack."

"So am I, Frank."

"I feel—I don't know—*renewed.*"

Warm air was blowing out of the heater now. A rim of frost was forming around the windshield. The heater and defrosters hissed, and the tire chains beat out a rapid thumping rhythm.

"What time is it?" I asked.

"Twenty minutes to five."

"We accomplished a lot back there, didn't we?"

"It's all right. It doesn't matter."

"It matters to me, Frank. The day got off to a rotten start."

"George will cool off."

"I don't care about George Stanger. I'm just saying that the whole business back there was depressing."

"Well, it's over now."

"Did you get the weather forecast?"

"It may clear up this afternoon. And with the temperature inversion it's a little warmer up in the high country than it is down here."

"Good enough."

"But there's a new storm moving down out of the northwest. More snow. It's supposed to arrive here early tomorrow."

"Beautiful," I said.

"Do you want to call it off, Jack?"

"Maybe later. Let's see what the conditions are up high."

Six miles from town we reached a fork in the highway; the highway curved to the left, and the right fork, a gravel road, angled in toward the mountains. The snow plows had been out all night and both roads were cleared. We took the right fork without slowing, and the rear end of the jeep started to slew around; it fishtailed a hundred yards before Frank managed to regain control.

"Scared?" Frank asked.

"Just keep your eyes on the road, Frank."

In the dim greenish light of the instrument panel, I could see that he was grinning. He removed his right hand from the steering wheel, clenched it into a fist and pounded me hard on the knee.

"You can't live forever," he said.

"I don't want to die in a machine, though."

"Why not? You machine-haters are all alike. How

would you rather die? Eaten by sharks? Of cancer? Starvation?"

"This is obviously multiple choice. Let me think about it."

"Just what do you chaps have against machines? A computer, for example."

"I've met some decent computers," I said.

"Sure. That's what you all say."

"I work with a swell computer down at the office."

"Okay, but did you ever invite him home for dinner?"

"You can't mix oil and water, Frank."

We drove another few miles, and now the road abruptly ended and a jeep trail continued on up through the forest of pine and spruce. It had not been plowed. Frank did not slacken speed; instead he pressed the accelerator down just before reaching the barrier of snow. There was a loud thump. The car fishtailed down the trail, losing speed. The headlight beams swung back and forth in a wide arc, lighting the trees on one side of the road and then swinging across to the other side and then back again. We nearly sideswiped a tree. Frank shifted the jeep into four-wheel drive. We kept going. The vehicle had a high center, but I could hear snow brushing against the underside. The road was defined only by a narrow strip of snow which wound through the trees. The trail rose steeply, and there were many sharp curves. Once it seemed that the jeep could not progress any farther, but Frank kept forcing it ahead. It was all very strange: the smooth ribbon of snow glowing brightly in the headlights; the shadowy trees; the straining of the engine.

"This is far enough," I said. "You don't want to get stuck."

"It's still a long hike from here to the cabin," he said. He was leaning forward, his face almost touching the windshield.

"We have time."

"Just a little farther."

We went on for another few minutes, until the road coiled into a series of sharp switchbacks. Frank turned off the ignition. The silence rushed in and swallowed us. There was a smell of exhaust and hot metal—the engine had overheated. Now the engine began to creak softly in the stillness.

"What a crazy idea," Frank said.

"Now you've got it," I told him.

I crawled over the seat into the rear and passed Frank his rucksack. We sorted out the equipment. Soon the windows were opaque with frost and glowed with a faint incandescence. Frank's head was a shadowy silhouette against the pale glow of the windshield. Our flashlights did not work. We had stupidly left them outside in the jeep, and the cold had drained the batteries.

I put my flashlight aside and removed a folding candle lantern from the rucksack. I slid it open, inserted a fresh candle and lit the wick. The flame grew, leaned away from my breath, settled into a thin wavering blade that filled the jeep with a soft white light. I adjusted the wind shield. The flame wasn't bright, but it would not be affected by wind or cold. It would do nicely. Often the oldest and simplest devices were the most trustworthy.

Last night I had cut eyeholes into my woolen stocking cap; now I pulled it down over my face. I could see all right, but there was an unpleasant smell and the itch of wool. I drew on my mittens, opened the door and stepped out into the throbbing silence. The snow came to my knees. I scooped up a double handful and tried to pack it into a snowball, but it was like trying to pack flour or dry sand. I reached into the rear seat of the jeep and got my rucksack and hoisted it up onto my back. It felt heavy. I adjusted the shoulder straps with my thumbs.

I looked around at the night. No stars; the overcast remained complete. A faint wind moved through the treetops with a sound like hushed breathing. I stamped my feet and beat my mittened hands together. I didn't feel the cold so much now as I anticipated feeling it later.

Frank got out of the jeep and stood quietly for a moment, looking around. "Cold," he said. "It's *cold,* Jack. My, my. Cold!"

"Let's go," I said.

"If the snow is knee-deep down here it'll be waist-deep in the high country."

"Yes. Come on, Frank, let's get moving."

"Eager, are you?" He reached into the jeep and dragged out his rucksack. I held it for him while he slipped his arms through the straps. He shrugged, adjusting the weight. "Okay," he said.

We got our skis and poles. Frank slung the rifle over his shoulder.

"Are you really going to take that thing, Frank?"

"We've been through that."

The noise of the car doors slamming was heavy and ugly in the fragile silence. I broke trail; Frank followed a few yards behind. My skis sank down six or eight inches before the snow compressed enough to bear my weight. It was easy going; the snow was dry and light and seemed no more substantial than mist. I set a fast pace. It was a long way to the Columbine Cabin. We would follow the old jeep road for another two miles and then strike off onto a forest path. The path wound steeply up through a narrow valley for five miles before reaching the meadows. And then another four miles to reach the cabin. So we had eleven miles to go, nearly all of it uphill.

The candle lanterns swung freely from our wrists. The light was adequate; two round glows that illuminated the undersides of the trees and sent quivering shadows back and forth over the ground.

When we reached the turn-off onto the forest path, Frank took over the lead. The path was a narrow winding tunnel beneath the overhanging pine and spruce and fir boughs. Snow sifted down. There was a scent of resin. The spherical candlelight threw vibrating shadows and brought out splashes of color, the green of the trees, our clothing. Everything else was stark black and white. A creek paralleled the path, but it was frozen and silent and covered with snow now. Beneath the snow the ice was like sculptured milk-white marble, frozen motion, a long solid twisting strip of falls and ripples and mushroom splashes. When a large body of water freezes, there is a thunderous crack: I enjoyed the whimsical notion that perhaps a creek makes snapping noises down its entire length when freezing, like a string of firecrackers detonating. Now, beneath the ice, there were channels of moving water, and trout finned head-on into the current. I wondered how they lasted out the winter; what they fed on, how they moved among the catacombs of ice.

We went on in silence. After about a half hour we rounded a sharp curve in the path and saw four elk. We stopped and they stopped. They were massive when seen so close. And perhaps the candlelight and the big shadows exaggerated their bulk. Two were bucks; their long spiky antlers looked trophy-sized. Eyes glowed in the light. I could smell them. We paused on the trail, perhaps fifteen feet apart, and then the biggest of the elk slowly turned and delicately picked its way up a brushy embankment. The others followed. They retreated slowly and with great dignity.

"Why didn't you kill them, Frank?" I asked.

"Shut up," he said.

We continued up the path. It rose more steeply now, crossing and recrossing the frozen creek. When the path emerged into a small clearing we stopped. Frank brushed the snow off a fallen tree and set up his Primus stove. I filled an aluminum saucepan with water. It seemed colder now that we had halted. I removed a mitten, reached down and sifted the snow through my fingers. The snow was hardly heavier than the air. My fingers were exposed for only a few seconds, but they had begun to stiffen from the cold.

"How is the snow?" Frank asked.

"Dry, light. And it's been so cold that the crystals are sort of interlocked—that gives it a little stability. It's good snow, Frank, but there's so much of it, and it's lying on a slick, icy base of old snow. There will be avalanches. I guarantee it."

"What about the notch?"

"I don't know. We'll take a look. Maybe it's already avalanched."

When the water boiled we made two cups of instant coffee with plenty of sugar. It was hot and sweet and gave me a lift.

We waited. The nylon of my jacket crackled in the cold. The trees made creaking and popping noises. It was a cruel night. It would be a cruel day.

SEVEN

Light came swiftly. One moment it was night, and then all at once we could distinguish features of the landscape which lay beyond the candle glow. The first light was like dark gray smoke, then it gradually faded hue by hue into a glossy pearl gray that drew color from the trees and the tumbled masses of rock. The atmosphere had a peculiar luminosity this morning; though it was neither bright nor clear, it seemed to glow with a secret, pale fire. It had a fish-belly color and a fish's wet shine. It was a dawn of portent, not in any mystical sense, but because such unusual atmospheric conditions almost always precede a radical change in the weather. Frank had mentioned an incoming storm. I guessed that today would be clear, cold, hard as a gem, but that the new storm would arrive before night.

We clamped on our skis, hoisted up our rucksacks and started off on the path through the forest. We were fairly high now, among bare white aspens. I looked up through the trees at the sky. There were a few thin rips in the cloud cover, and the blue sky shone through. The light increased but did not lose its curious luminous quality. The path through the trees grew steeper, tacking up the hills in tight switchbacks. And then the trees gradually thinned out until those which remained were small, gnarled and dwarfed, permanently leaning away from the prevailing winds. We were at about eleven thousand feet.

We went on until we reached the narrow V-notch entrance to the cirque. The notch was no more than one hundred yards wide at the base, and mountain slopes rose steeply on either side. It was a very dangerous area.

"I'll go through first," I said. "Watch me carefully all the way. If an avalanche hits and I get buried, move your ass."

"Aw, for Christ's sake, Jack."

"You remain here until I wave my arms."

"Jack . . ."

"Shut up. I know a little more about these things than you do. We'll move one at a time."

"Jack," he said in a disgusted tone, "you've been spooked. You're no good up here anymore."

I started through the notch. I tried for a smooth, swift cross-country ski rhythm, poling hard, stretching out, breathing deeply, and I kept to the same pace even after fatigue dimmed my vision and deadened the muscles of my arms and legs. My shoulders felt close to paralysis. It was difficult to sustain hard physical effort at this altitude unless you were in absolutely top condition; there simply was not enough oxygen to fuel the muscles and brain otherwise. The notch widened, opened into the great bowl.

I kept going until I thought I was safe, and then I went another fifty feet to punish my body. I turned and looked back. I had gone three hundred yards and gained perhaps two hundred feet of altitude. Frank, far below me, was just a brightly colored speck among the last of the dwarf trees. I waved, and he started skiing up toward me. He did not seem to be in any hurry. I half-hoped a mountain would fall on him.

He was right, though; I had been spooked by avalanches. I had been most seriously spooked two years ago when the avalanche control team—myself, Ralph Brace and Terry Braden—had been out bombing some potentially dangerous slopes after a storm. We had thrown half a dozen canisters of explosive down on a short, very steep trail called Abomination, and it had not avalanched. We thought it was probably safe. It was my turn to ski a trail; the others would follow one at a time. It was our procedure, and a matter of personal and team honor, to ski every slope that we declared open to the public.

I had got almost halfway down when I heard a sound, a faint hissing, like a sound of boiling water being poured into a teacup. I looked back over my shoulder and saw a smoky white tide rushing down on me. It looked as if the whole upper half of the mountain had broken off. Little balls of snow bounced past me. An oval mass of snow the size of an automobile came bounding and spinning past me to the left and then suddenly disintegrated into crystalline powder which sparkled blindingly in the sunlight. Then I was swept away. I tried to do all the things one is supposed to do in such circumstances: I dropped my ski poles to free my hands; I remained calm; I made breast-stroke swimming motions with my arms to stay on the surface; I held my breath, refusing to breathe the snow particles. And when I knew that I was going under, I brought my hands up in front of my face to create a small breathing pocket. I was knocked off my feet and tumbled down the mountain and driven under, and the motion continued for a time and then ceased.

I felt as though I were encased in plaster. Although the snow was dry and powdery, it consolidated immediately after the motion stopped. I have an unreasonable terror of enclosed places. This was horror beyond description, and I could not wholly subdue my panic. There was snow in my mouth and nose, and cold snow pressing against my face. I thrashed around with my hands and forearms, trying to enlarge my breathing pocket. I succeeded.

Now I had to survive until the others found me. It was impossible to dig my way out; the snow was too hard. Even if I could, I had no notion of where the surface was, and so I might tunnel upward or parallel to the slope. I did not feel cold. I was not in pain. I reminded myself that men had survived for hours beneath the snow.

We always trailed a thirty-foot length of red cord behind us while on avalanche duty. If a part of the cord had remained above the surface, they could follow it down to where I lay. I knew there was a good chance, if my heart did not quit, if I did not consume all the available oxygen in paroxysms of panic breathing.

I was told later that I was only under the snow for about fifteen minutes. Of course it seemed much longer than that; it seemed an enormous period of time, equal to all the years I had lived before. It was very strange: I could hear Braden's and Ralph's voices, could feel their weight above me, but they could not hear my own muffled shouts. I heard Braden say he believed they were searching in the wrong place. His few words almost killed me; I almost gave up when I heard them.

They dug me out from under five feet of snow. A few inches of the colored nylon cord had remained above the surface. They dug a pit with their skis, freed a space around my head and then excavated my body. I was in shock; I had a touch of frostbite on my cheeks, and my heartbeat was abnormally slow. After two days of rest I was as strong as ever physically, but the bad dreams continued for a long time and occasionally visit me now.

I had been spooked by my brief Lazarus act, but also by other avalanches that I'd seen and heard about. A big avalanche is as destructive as a tornado; more, since it can destroy in three or four ways. One can strip a great forest slope as easily as a man shaves off his morning beard: all you see in the spring when the snow has melted are some splintered, uprooted stumps, wood and rock debris, and thousands of great trees scattered about in tangled piles. Often, hurricane winds of compressed air precede a dry snow avalanche, and the snow cloud itself is followed by a vacuum which exerts a powerful suction. Once, while working with the State Highway Department, I had seen a rotary snow plow picked up by such a wind and hurled a hundred feet. I had been operating a howitzer, lobbing shells onto a loaded slope from a distance of two miles, and when the slide started I'd quickly grabbed my binoculars. The avalanche had divided into two prongs, then converged, and the snow plow, which had been left in what I believed to be a safe place, had been lifted and thrown as easily as an angry child might throw his toy truck. A really big avalanche, the kind that occurs in the Himalayas or the Andes or Alaska, could probably generate winds strong enough to toss a locomotive engine across the Mississippi.

No, I did not like them. I did not understand them. There were only three basic types of avalanches: dry snow, wet snow, and slab; but each category had subcategories which were determined by such variables as sun, wind, rate of snowfall, depth of snow, terrain (the steepness of the slope, its general conformation—smooth or gullied, concave or convex, forested or bare—lee slope or windward), the temperature of the different snow layers, and the air temperature, the base, the moisture content of the snow, the composition of the snow in its many strata . . .

Just about the time that I became known around the state as an avalanche "expert," I quit that job, because I could not take the responsibility for life and property while remaining so ignorant of my adversary. I told my superiors in the Forest Service either to send me to Davos, Switzerland, for a year or so of study, or to hire a genuine expert. They hired an expert, a man from Davos. He does a good job, much better than I could have done, and when he makes a mistake he does so on the basis of the most recent scientific evidence.

Frank was almost out of the danger zone now. He moved lazily, paused to adjust a ski pole strap, continued.

I inverted my own ski pole and pushed it handle-down into the snow: it sank almost to the basket before striking a harder layer of snow beneath. Nearly five feet of snow had fallen here within the last twenty-four hours. More in the really high country.

Frank finally reached me. He was not even breathing hard. He grinned, nodded.

"I wanted to save something for the descent this afternoon," he said.

"So did I, Frank."

We climbed a gentle slope for about half a mile, and then the grade steepened and we were forced to herring-bone the remaining hundred and fifty yards to the top of the hill. Wind burned our faces. We had a spectacular view in every direction now. The sudden beauty was almost shocking after all the gloom of the dark cold morning hours, the arduous climb, the overcast, our partial reluctance to be here. But then we reached the top of the hill and were ambushed by space and static power. White mountains exploded into the sky. It looked as if there had been a terrible explosion, and as if, just as the uprising earth had reached its greatest velocity, it had frozen. It was a massive, heavy scene, but fluid, too, as though the power remained and it all might resume motion as we watched. The dark, high-altitude sky was streaked with ragged streamers of mist.

Frank laughed. "Okay," he said. "All right."

Each mountain peak was different from the others; each had a separate mood and character. They reached off into the misty blue nothing. That snowy peak dipped down into a saddle which rose to another peak, and so on, and it continued beyond the limits of my vision. Up there, on the summits and ridges, long white clouds of snow were blowing from the northwest to the southeast. Sunlight flashed iridescently through the snow plumes. I was excited, confused; I wanted to be higher. You could walk through the sky forever.

I yearned for something unknown, but I felt good. I had had this night and the dawn; I had had the snapping cold and the deep powder snow and the long ski in alongside the frozen creek; and the elk; and this. The unpleasantness with George Stanger and Tom Horne meant nothing. All that seemed insignificant now in the vast cold white silence. The mountains, the sky, assured me that it had no importance. And for a few minutes I was not afraid of avalanches. It seemed to me that nothing really bad could happen to you here. You could die, but death itself had no more importance than the descent of a single snowflake. I remained aware that death was up here, but I believed that life and death were like close sisters—you couldn't become a lover of the beautiful one without meeting the other. I realized that I might find death in the mountains, maybe today, but just once; and I had found life in the same place a hundred times.

Frank was scanning the country before us with the telescopic sight on his rifle. “I think I see smoke,” he said.

“Where?”

“Right about where the cabin is located.”

“I don’t see anything.”

“Jack, I’m pretty sure . . .”

“Maybe it’s just the mist.”

“No, it’s smoke all right.”

“So they found the cabin,” I said.

“Right.” He lowered the rifle and offered it to me. “Here, take a look.”

“No, never mind, I can see the smoke now. I was looking too far west before. Well, Christ, Frank, they made it.”

We looked out onto the Columbine Meadows. It was a big horseshoe-shaped area of snow-covered alpine tundra enclosed by two chains of mountains. To our left, the Mt. Wolf Massif, a long, rugged ridge system, with the Wolf, at 14,191 feet, placed almost precisely at the center. On our right, another high, long ridge with two peaks over 14,000 feet; and straight ahead, bridging the gap, was a 12,000-foot col. Beyond the col lay the ski mountain; below that mountain, the town.

The basin, Columbine Meadows, had been carved out by glaciers thousands of years before, and erosion was slowly continuing the process. It was a beautiful place during the brief summer season, sun-flooded, with long yellow tundra grass and lupines and blue and yellow columbines, and big brown marmots which whistled from among the rocks. Now, though, it was a cold, sun-blinding two-dimensional expanse of white.

"I'm going to take a couple of pictures," I said.

"How long will that take?"

"Not more than five minutes."

"Hurry, will you?" Frank said. "The wind is cold."

I took a reading of the light, made the proper lens adjustments, and took six shots, one of the Wolf and its long sparkling snow plume, then several more of the encircling ridges and summits, and then the final one looking down over the Columbine Meadows.

"Frank," I said, "I'll ski down first. I want to take a picture looking up over my tracks, with you up here silhouetted against the sky. Then you move over about fifty feet and ski down through clean snow, and I'll try to get a couple of good action shots."

"Jack, it's damned cold in this wind."

"Maybe your picture will make the cover of *Colorado* magazine. Or *Empire.*"

"Yeah?"

"Sure. This is the perfect story for them."

"Okay, but hurry, will you?"

"Try to ski with a little class, Frank."

"It's hard to ski with class in touring gear."

"Finish up with a telemark, about ten feet from the camera."

He nodded. "While you're gone, I'll practice making my jaw square. Do you want me to grin?"

"No, Frank, I think the square jaw will be enough."

"I have good teeth."

"Marvelous teeth, but the square jaw and those great ivory wedges would be unbearably heroic in Kodachrome."

"Women are attracted and confused by the paradox of my soft, suffering eyes and brutal mouth. They tell conflicting stories."

"I know, Frank."

"Nobility and cruelty."

I tucked the camera back inside my jacket, closed the snaps, slipped my mittened hands through the ski pole straps and pushed off the rim of the hill. The snow was very deep, and I moved slowly at first, almost coming to a stop three or four times, but then the incline steepened and gravity grabbed me and started pulling. My speed seemed to increase geometrically. I was hardly moving at all, and then I had gained enough momentum so that I did not have to pole, and then suddenly the wind was cold on my face, my eyes watered behind the sunglasses, and I was nearly out of control. The faster I went, the higher my skis rode in the snow. The snow was thigh-deep; knee-deep; and then my ski tips rose up through the surface like a pair of high-prowed boats in a foaming, billowy sea. I stem-Christied, traversed the hill, stemmed again, gaining confidence, thinking a fraction of a second ahead of my reflexes. I sat back over the skis, unweighted, and tried a parallel turn which was shaky but worked, and then I cut loose down the fall line. My ski tips appeared again; I was skimming the foam, nearly weightless. There was a sensation in my stomach as when an elevator suddenly begins to drop.

My eyes were streaming tears. Nothing but gently undulating whiteness; I left the scars in the snow behind me. I checked my speed with two short heel thrusts, tried it again; and then either my equipment or my technique failed, and I was rolling down through the cold, feather-soft snow.

After the tumbling and sliding stopped, I lay quiet for a moment, waiting for pain. No pain, just the downy softness of the snow and the beginning of a cool wetness on my neck and wrists. I slowly dug myself from the snow, stood up, slipped and fell down, rose again. Frank, nicely posed against the sky, laughed at me.

I fixed my bindings and skied down the remainder of the hill and then turned and took a couple of photographs of my imperfect tracks. They told a story, too, one that all skiers could identify.

Frank came down through fresh snow, skiing beautifully, and finished with an absolutely perfect telemark. His jaw was square; his grin was enormous, artificial, ridiculous.

We continued on up toward the refuge. The meadows gradually widened into a huge bowl surrounded by steep, concave mountain slopes. Sunlight was reflected and re-reflected off the floor and walls of the snow bowl, and the whole area glittered and blazed with a cold white light. The sun looked like a Fourth of July sparkler.

We went on, and for a moment I imagined that I was standing on the corniced, wind-ripped summit of the Wolf, looking down through the snow plume at Frank and myself, a couple of tiny specks against the ocean of white (two fleas in a bathtub was the image that came to mind), crawling slowly toward a thin, spiraling column of gray woodsmoke.

We paused for a cigarette. The smoke was close now, although we still could not see the snow-drifted cabin.

Frank cupped his hands. “Hello,” he called in the deep, chesty, resonant voice that carries well in the mountain air. “Hello.”

He turned to me. “Their fire is going to feel good.”

“Yes, but we can’t stay long.”

“Why not?”

“The snow isn’t getting any better, Frank.”

“The omnipresent voice of doom,” he said. He cupped his hands again, lifted his chin “Doom,” he shouted. “Doooooom. Doooooom. Can you hear me? *Doooooom!*” The echoes were just low humming sounds, like the vibration of a guitar’s G string.

“Let’s go,” I said.

He threw his cigarette into the snow. “Let’s go,” he repeated. “Doom. Let’s go. Doom.”

EIGHT

We went on, and when we were close enough to smell the woodsmoke, the proportions and some of the details of the cabin emerged out of the uniform sparkling whiteness. Before, it had looked like just another large snowdrift, but now I could see the straight dark line of the eaves, the mottled rocks and mortar just below the eaves, a few panes of frosted window glass, and, not far above eye-level, the squarish rock chimney thrusting up through the snow. The cabin was more than half-buried.

We skied to within forty feet of the cabin, and then the head and torso of a man materialized and began floating from left to right across our field of vision.

When we were closer, we could see that he was standing in a trench that had been shoveled out of the snow. The trench slanted downward and ended at the cabin's heavy oak door.

"The cabin is occupied," he said.

We stopped and looked down at him.

"We'll be leaving here after lunch," he said. "It's all yours then."

"Is it?" Frank said. "Well, you don't mind if we come in and warm ourselves by your fire, do you?"

"Yes. We were here first. You can have the place around one."

Frank looked at me. "Jack," he said.

"Yes, Frank."

"How cold do you think it is?"

"Oh, I'd guess about fifteen below zero."

"There is a wind," Frank said.

"Yes, I believe there is a light wind."

"What would you estimate the wind speed to be?"

"Frank, this is only a rough estimate, but right here, where we're standing, the wind is probably blowing at around eight miles per hour. Eight to ten miles per hour, I'd say."

"That sounds okay. Fifteen below zero, an eight-mile-per-hour wind. What is the wind-chill factor, Jack?"

The young man was watching us suspiciously.

"Frank," I said, "the effective temperature is probably around thirty degrees below zero."

"It is now eleven ten A.M.," Frank said.

"That isn't bad. We have to wait for only one hour and fifty minutes at the equivalent of thirty degrees below zero."

"This is a hilarious routine," the man said. He was a big kid, one of those blond, tanned California mutants, a new subspecies that has recently swarmed up from the beaches to the mountains. He was built like a cartoon hero, Joe Palooka or Li'l Abner, with enormous shoulders which tapered down to an absurdly narrow waist. He was not wearing a coat, just boots, stretch pants and a heavy green knit sweater with white reindeer across the breast. But he did not appear chilled; he breathed big clouds of vapor and looked at us with an expression somewhere between irony and hostility. He exuded health. He was big, strong, with greenish eyes and a blond Viking beard. He had a way of looking at you that was more than half a physical challenge.

"You're Erich Kemp," I said.

"That's right."

"You must have had some luck to find the cabin yesterday during the storm."

He didn't answer; he just looked at me. His gaze was hard, unblinking, insolent. A macho.

"Okay," I said. "Get your friends and we'll ski down out of here together."

"We're going to ski down after lunch," he said. "You can do whatever you like."

"Kemp," Frank said, "we're with the Forest Service. We've come up here to collect you and your friends."

"We aren't the type to be collected," he said.

"There's some avalanche danger," Frank said. "And there is a lunatic running around. He killed a lot of people yesterday, and he might show up here today."

"You two make yourselves comfortable out here," Kemp said. "We'll be out in a couple of hours."

"I can't believe this character," Frank said.

"Kemp," I said.

"Yeah?"

"You are on land administered by the U.S. Forest Service. We are members of the Forest Service."

"I heard your partner mention that."

"We have full police powers here."

"You can begin enforcing your police powers at one o'clock."

"Look," Frank said. "We're not trying to hassle you; we just—"

"You aren't hassling me at all."

"You can cooperate or be arrested," Frank told him, his voice rising.

"Are you going to shoot me with that big bad rifle while I eat lunch?" Kemp asked contemptuously.

"No, goddamn it, I'm just trying to tell you that we have the authority to—"

"Stick your authority," he said quietly.

"Frank," I said.

"Huh?" He looked at me.

"Move away from the eave, will you?"

"What?"

"There's five feet of snow on the roof, and a fire inside the cabin is melting the snow, and it's all going to come down sooner or later. You don't want to be standing there when a ton of snow slides off."

"Oh, for Christ's sake, Jack!"

"Kemp," I said, "do you refuse to obey our instructions?"

"That's right."

"You are under arrest for disobeying the lawful orders of Forest Service personnel while in the jurisdiction of the United States Forest Service, Department of Agriculture. You have the right to remain silent. If you choose to discuss this incident you may, at any time, refuse to continue. You have the right to obtain the services of a lawyer. Your lawyer may be present during any interrogation. If you cannot afford a lawyer, you will be provided with one free of charge. Anything you say may be used in court against you."

He grinned at me, turned and started down the trench.

"Kemp," I said, "you have ten minutes in which to decide whether or not you really want to resist arrest. If you *do* resist, we shall subdue you with all the required, reasonable force."

Kemp entered the cabin and slammed the door shut behind him.

Frank and I stood quietly for a moment.

"You sounded pretty pompous," Frank said.

"I guess so."

"Where did you get all that stuff?"

"I saw it on TV."

"He wasn't terribly impressed."

"I noticed that."

"Well," Frank said. "He's an arrogant one, all right."

I nodded.

"Well, hell."

Someone inside the cabin rubbed a clear spot in the frost, and behind it I could see the pale blur of a face.

"Jack, he is one big son of a bitch, and there's another guy inside who may be ten feet tall, with fists as big as your head and ball-peen hammers for knuckles. Are we really going to go inside and subdue them?"

"Frank, move away from the roof."

"Yes, father." He sidestepped a few yards. "Jack?"

"We'll wait ten minutes and then go into the cabin and try to run a bluff on him."

"You tried a bluff. It worked beautifully."

"Then we'll just try to persuade the other two to come down with us."

"What if they get their backs up like Kemp and refuse?"

"Then we'll go down alone."

"Are you really going to press charges?"

"If they survive. You bet."

"Maybe we did come on a little too strong, Jack."

"There's no way we could have approached that kid. Can you feature it? Telling us to wait almost two hours while they enjoyed a leisurely lunch?"

"He's a porcupine, all right. Are you keeping track of the time?"

"No."

"We'll start now. Twenty minutes."

"Ten, Frank."

He grinned and leaned over his ski poles.

My feet were cold, my face was sunburned and windchapped, and I was beginning to get a headache from the intense sun glare. It was foolish to be standing here like a pair of stuffed herons, while a few yards away there was a warm, dry room where we could rest in comfort; but it seems that in any kind of angry confrontation between men, some primitive rules are devised without anyone's being consciously aware of it, and so for the time being, at least, the cabin was Kemp's territory, and the rest of the area, the cold, snowy part, belonged to Frank and me. It was stupid, but I felt obliged to give Kemp his ten minutes before we invaded his den.

Frank unslung his rifle and looked through the telescopic sight at the high rims and summits which encircled us. He started on the Wolf and slowly twisted around until he was aiming over the cabin roof. He lowered the rifle.

"Some huge cornices are building up on the Wolf's ridges," he said.

"You were looking at the lee slope," I said. "A hell of a lot of snow is blowing over from the windward side of the mountains."

"You've made me nervous, Jack."

"Did you see any sign of small slides? Anything that might indicate the snow is getting unstable?"

"No."

The cabin door opened and a girl walked up the trench, stopped, shaded her eyes with a palm and looked up at us. She was pretty, with long auburn hair, long-lashed greenish eyes with a faint oval slant, like a cat's eyes, prominent, sculpted cheekbones and jawline. She seemed undecided between anger and appeasement.

"Hello," Frank said, smiling at her. "I'm Frank Treblene and this is Jack Marty."

She hesitated, looking first at Frank, then at me. "My name is Karen Bright," she said.

"Hi, Karen," Frank said, still smiling.

"Are you really going to arrest Erich?" she asked. Frank's friendly greeting had apparently decided her in favor of appeasement.

"Not if he will agree to come with us now," Frank said.

"He said you two were very arrogant."

"We thought he was pretty arrogant himself, miss."

"Erich is very proud."

"Other people have pride, too," I said. "Did he tell you that you're in avalanche danger?"

"He said we're too far from the mountains, that an avalanche wouldn't reach us."

"He's wrong."

"Well . . ."

"And did he tell you that there is also a berserk sniper somewhere in the vicinity, and if he sees you he's liable to shoot out your green eyes?"

She paused, biting her lower lip. "He said something about that."

"Get your things ready," I told her. "We're going down."

"Jack," Frank said, "take it easy."

"Frank, we just haven't got the time to treat these prima donnas with diplomacy. Ninety-nine out of a hundred people would be grateful to us; they'd jump. Look around you, man; the sun and wind are working on the snow. It's all going to come down sooner or later, maybe while we're standing here trying to persuade these exquisitely sensitive people to come with us."

The girl was watching me.

"Miss Bright. We're with the Forest Service, and we have come here specifically because we believed you three might be in danger. We didn't know if you'd be able to find the cabin during yesterday's storm. And there *is* considerable avalanche danger. And there *is* a sniper around, a young man who has gone so totally nuts that he'd rather shoot you than make love to you. Am I making any sort of impression on you?"

"Please," she said. "Let me go inside and talk to Erich and Paul."

"Make it quick, will you?"

"Please," she said. She went down the trench and entered the cabin.

"Very pretty," Frank said.

"Yeah."

"Did you notice that she has the slightest trace of a lisp? Very charming."

"Charming, Frank."

He grinned. "I liked that line about how Ralph would rather shoot her than make love to her. Do you think that's true?"

"Yes."

"Scary. Really scary."

I removed my skis and stuck them into the snow. "I'll go in and talk to them," I said.

"I'll come with you," Frank said. "You might need some muscle."

"No. If they're stubborn about it we'll go down alone."

I waded through the deep snow to the trench, went down the trench and through the door into the cabin. I could not see well at first; the room was dim, almost black in comparison to the sun and snow glitter of the outside. Kemp and the girl were in the center of the room; just two dark shadows, one big and the other small.

"Have you decided?" I asked.

"Just a few more minutes, please," the girl said.

There were four small windows in the cabin, about twelve by twelve inches, one placed high on each of the four stone walls. The east window, the sun side, had been totally buried by the snowdrifts. The three other windows were frosted over and did not admit much light. A mound of orange coals glowed in the fireplace across the room. The fireplace was not drawing properly; the room was filled with a smoky haze.

I could see a little better now. Kemp and the girl were standing close together, whispering. Beyond them I could see the other man, Murphy, sitting on a pile of wood in the corner. He was watching me.

I glanced around the cabin. It was small, twenty-four feet by sixteen, with a steeply slanting roof and closely spaced ceiling beams as thick as telephone poles. The roof had to be extremely strong in order to support the mass of winter snow. The walls were strong, too, eighteen inches thick, made out of big rocks taken from the lower talus slopes of the Wolf. I had supervised construction of the cabin three years ago. The Forest Service had provided me with a small crew of summer employees, mostly college students, and we had built the cabin in six weeks, good time considering the logistical problems. I had deviated from the blueprints in several areas, exceeding the specifications, because I knew better than the architect what these high mountain winds, snows, and temperature variations can do to a structure that is not sturdily built. The cabin was thick, massive, solid—and impermanent. It had lasted three years. It might last another three, or five, or maybe even ten, but one day, when the conditions were just so, an avalanche was going to come boiling down off the Wolf, and afterwards all that would remain would be a pile of rubble.

There was a wooden picnic table and some benches in the room, bunks built onto the walls, shelves, cupboards, a couple of kerosene lanterns. I walked past Kemp and the girl and stood in front of the fireplace. Paul Murphy looked at me. He was a tall, thin young man with a wispy blond moustache and round, wire-rimmed glasses.

"What are you going to do?" I asked him.

He cleared his throat. "Whatever Erich and Karen decide."

"They always make your decisions for you?"

He did not answer.

"A troika, huh, Paul? Utilize your vote, man."

He started to speak, shrugged, turned away. He seemed to be a sullen kid, but I guessed that he was just very shy.

"All right, Mr.—?" the girl said.

I turned and went to the center of the room. "Jack," I said.

"We've decided to go with you."

"Good. Let's get moving, then."

"Listen," Kemp said. "I'm not leaving here because I'm afraid of you and your buddy, or because I'm afraid to get arrested. I'm coming because Karen has asked me to."

"Fine. Whatever."

"Just so you have that straight."

"You've made it clear. Now, where is your skiing gear?"

"We left our things outside yesterday, against the wall," the girl said. "The snow has covered them."

"Someone better dig them out."

Kemp went over to the door, opened it and went outside.

The girl was looking at me. There was a short silence.

"Look," I said. "Don't let this spoil your day."

"Well, it really hasn't been very pleasant, you know."

"I know. But it's a fine day, and you won't get many chances to ski powder snow like this. Let's all try to enjoy the run down."

She nodded.

"Frank and I will follow a couple hundred yards behind you if you like. You'll probably enjoy it more that way."

"No, no, that isn't necessary. You and your friend might as well ski with us."

NINE

I dropped my rucksack in a corner, got the two-gallon aluminum bucket from the cupboard, and went outside for some snow to put on the fire. The cold air tasted deliciously sweet after breathing the too-warm, smoky haze inside the cabin. I walked up the trench and stopped, squinting against the glare. Frank was looking toward the northeast through his rifle telescope. He swung the barrel to the right a few degrees, then back again to the left, and then he held it there.

"Frank," I said, "we're all going down now."

"I know; that's what the big guy told me."

I scooped a bucketful of snow from the wall of the trench. "Why don't you help him dig out their skiing gear?"

"Jack," he said, and there was a sound like the snapping of a dry stick of wood. Frank's head seemed to swell like a balloon. That is how it appeared. His hat went flying, his hair bristled like the fur on a cat's back, his head grew large, misshapen, and a misty halo of blood formed in the air as his head came apart. I remember the blood halo, and the silence, most clearly. After the initial wood-snapping sound, it was absolutely quiet for a couple of seconds as a ruby mist, glowing in the sunlight, bloomed around his head. His head snapped back, swelling and fragmenting, smoking blood; he bent backwards at the waist; his knees buckled and he fell into the snow.

I did not understand; I could not evaluate my perceptions. There were specks of blood on my hands and jacket, and a peppering of blood in the bucket of snow. And then, finally, I heard the sharp, echoing crack of the rifle, and I understood.

Kemp, out of sight around the corner of the cabin, said, "What? What?" And then he was hit. There was a dull but still faintly resonating sound, like a fist blow to the chest; the expulsion of air in a long, almost weary sigh, and then the silence again. One second, two seconds . . . the whipcrack of the rifle, followed by descending, muffled echoes.

The bucket was torn out of my hand and flung against the cabin wall. I felt pain in my wrist, elbow, and shoulder joints. Was I shot? I could not act, I could not sort out the various stimuli. I was reacting to the sound of the shots rather than to their earlier impact. Confusion, numbness, as every alternative was canceled by an opposite alternative. The bucket was ripped from my hand, and I could not move until I heard the delayed report. I dove headfirst down the trench and belly-slid down the icy ramp. My head struck the base of the door. I looked up for the door handle and saw a white starburst magically appear on the rock wall a couple of feet above me and to the right. Rock, or lead fragments, stung my cheek. Then the door was opened from the inside and I slithered through, shouting, "Get down! Get down!"

The door was slammed shut and bolted. Paul Murphy, frowning, his eyes round, the pupils completely encircled by white, was staring down at me.

"On the floor!" I screamed.

The girl was rubbing a clear spot in the frosted window with her palm.

"Get away from the window! Get down, get down!"

She looked over at me, her face impassive, a bland mask, and then she very slowly settled to her hands and knees.

The window exploded with a brittle crack, and frosted glass shards showered the room.

Murphy was still on his feet. I reached out, grasped his ankles and pulled, and he toppled, fell loosely, without the tension or quickness that reflexes provide—he was, in a way, sleeping now as I had been asleep while outside. Murphy fell hard, lay there for a moment and then, suddenly awakened, scurried across the floor on his hands and knees to the cupboards beneath the kitchen workbench. He pulled open the double doors and somehow squeezed himself inside that small space, doubling up like an out-of-use marionette, and then he closed the doors from the inside.

The girl was now lying prone at the juncture of wall and floor. I could feel cold air coming in through the broken window. A bullet came in through the window and ricocheted off the floor, the back wall and then a side wall. I crawled past the door and fitted myself into the corner. The stone was cold against my cheek and had a dry, musty odor. I tried to make myself very small. It occurred to me later that I might have covered the girl's body with my own, to protect her from the ricochets; but I had seen Frank's head explode and heard Kemp's dying sigh, and I was too panicked to even consider daring my life in a chivalrous gesture.

Ralph Brace kept shooting in through the window. He knew that the floor and walls were stone and that the bullets would whine around the room like angry insects. They did; they whined, cracked, buzzed, and I was convinced that they possessed an intelligence of their own and were deliberately hunting us down like infuriated bees. The girl was silent. Murphy, behind the cupboard doors, was making soft, crooning sounds. I could feel the cold stones against my cheek, smell my sweat, hear my rapid breathing. My back was sprayed with bullet fragments. There was no pain, just the realization that something bad had happened to my body and that I would not learn exactly what until the shock and adrenalin wore off. The air hummed. And then it was quiet in the room, although I could hear the distant crack of the rifle.

"Don't move," I said. My voice was muffled by the walls.

I guessed that Ralph had paused to reload his rifle. We waited. There was a sour-cream taste in my mouth.

I could not get enough air; I felt as though I had been running for miles.

Ralph resumed shooting, and again the room screamed and hummed with ricocheting bullets. The pause had given me time in which to regain partial control of myself. I felt slightly calmer now; I could think. We would not die, not yet. Ralph was probably using soft-nosed or hollow-point hunting ammunition, and the bullets were shattering on impact. We were being sprayed by the fragments.

Finally the shooting stopped. I could smell rock dust and smoke from the fire. I waited two or three minutes, kneeling and facing into the corner like a punished child, and then I slowly turned and rose to my feet. My legs were weak; my knee hinges could hardly support my weight. I was physically exhausted, and yet I had done nothing more than crawl across the floor and crouch against the wall. I placed my palm against the wall.

There was blood in the girl's hair. I walked over to her and knelt on the floor. I separated the strands of her hair, looking for the source of the blood, and found several small cuts in her scalp. She did not move during my examination. I grasped her shoulder and rolled her over onto her back. She stared at me.

"Am I badly hurt?" she asked.

"No."

"My head . . ."

"Superficial cuts. Do you have pain elsewhere?"

"No. Will he start shooting again?"

"I don't know."

"Oh, God," she said.

"I think you can sit up now if you want to."

"I don't want to yet. Erich—is he dead?"

"He was hit."

"But is he dead?"

"I don't know. Probably."

"Oh, God," she said again.

She was in shock; her face was very pale, and when I touched her cheek it felt cool and moist.

"Where is Paul?"

"He's in the cupboard," I said.

It was four months before I could laugh about Paul Murphy folding himself in sections inside the cupboard and closing the doors behind, but she smiled then. It was a faint, brief smile, but it was genuine. I felt great affection for her. I didn't know her, but we were allies, and temporarily as close as two people can be—allies in the exclusive club of death.

"What if that man comes for us?"

"The door is bolted, and it's very heavy."

"But the windows!"

"He would have to stick his rifle through a window to shoot us. It's very dark in here compared to outside, and he wouldn't be able to see us at first. Maybe I could get the rifle away from him."

"Do you think so, really?"

"Yes, I really do. But he'll probably wait until dark. He's a long distance away and he'd have to cross open spaces to reach us. For all he knows, we may be armed."

She slowly sat up and leaned her back against the wall. She closed her eyes. "I'm so weak."

"Yes."

She opened her eyes. "Your face is bleeding."

I ran my fingertips over my face, felt the slick blood and a number of small cuts. "Lead fragments. I think I have some in my back, too."

"Paul?" the girl said. "Paul!"

There was no response.

"Maybe Paul is hurt."

"Murphy," I said.

"What?" A muffled, sullen voice.

"Come out of there."

"No," he said.

"Why does that man want to hurt us?" she asked.

"I don't know. He's crazy."

"What are we going to do?"

"We can't do anything except wait."

The cupboard doors opened and Murphy unfolded himself in sections—he seemed to possess a half dozen more joints than ordinary people—and he looked at us and said, "Karen, I want to go home now."

TEN

"Murphy," I said, "go and sit directly beneath the south window."

"No," he said sullenly, not looking at me.

"He'll have to break the window in order to use his rifle. If you hear the window break, rise up and grab the rifle barrel from below. Hold on to it until I reach you."

"Karen," he said querulously, "I don't want to do it."

"You must do as he says, Paul," she said quietly.

"I don't want to."

"What's the matter with him?" I asked the girl.

"Paul is a very talented, very sensitive musician."

"That isn't an explanation."

"Paul," the girl said, "go over to the window."

"No."

"Move!" I said. "Or I'll get up and kick you across the room."

He looked at me, saw that I meant it, and slowly and reluctantly rolled to his hands and knees and crawled across the room. When he reached the wall below the window he turned and looked at me again. I nodded.

"Karen, you take the west window."

"Okay."

"I'll take the broken one. The east window is buried beneath the snow, and so we won't have to worry about it."

"Do you think he'll come after us?" she asked.

"He'll come," I said. "Probably not until after dark, but we have to be prepared."

She crawled across the floor and stationed herself beneath the thickly frosted west window. I slid over until I could feel a cold draft from the broken north window. We waited. I hoped that if Ralph came soon he would attack through my window or the girl's. I did not trust Murphy to react; he was in a kind of daze, halfway between apathy and a child's spiteful sulk, and he would not be any good in the crisis. The girl seemed all right. She had the courage, and with a little time in which to regain control of her emotions, she might have the reflexes.

I tried to figure out what Ralph Brace would do. He had seen Frank's rifle, and so he would probably assume all of us were armed. He would think we were members of the big manhunt, here to close off his exit to the south. He would wait.

Ralph—how could I have failed to see the sickness in him? True, we had not associated with each other during the past year, but the sickness, the hatred, the fear and murder must have been present in him during the prior two years when we'd been friends. Why hadn't I seen them? I remembered reading somewhere that paranoid schizophrenics were capable of behaving quite normally in areas that did not touch upon their system of delusion and obsession. If that was true, and Ralph was a paranoid schizophrenic (Ormond, though, had called him a sociopath), and my relationship with him lay *outside* the "system" . . . Still, there must have been clues, nuances of behavior that I had missed.

I had told Ormond that Ralph was "cheerful." That was basically true, but there had been times when he was anxious and tense—"Oh, I'm feeling a little uptight today," he'd say when you questioned him—so tense sometimes that his voice became choky and his face looked pale and frozen. Yet, who is not occasionally anxious and tense in these times? But generally Ralph was relaxed, especially up in the mountains. He laughed often then; there was a real joy in him.

I had told Ormond that Ralph had sometimes been reckless on our avalanche patrols. Yes, but not in a way that seemed morbid, a denial of life. I had believed it to be exuberance. It had been exuberance when Terry Braden or I did something similarly foolish: there are moments when life is so overwhelmingly wonderful that you are tempted to visit death and pay your disrespects.

What had he been doing during his isolation of the past year?

I visualized him brooding in the solitary confinement of his room (but is the room filthy and stinking, or immaculately clean as before?).

I see him haunted by obscure insults and snubs, tortured by a glance, a whisper, a laugh. In seclusion all the night and most of the day, avoiding friends—tormentors? Thinking, thinking, penetrating their devious schemes and devising counter-stratagems of his own.

Seeing through their masks. Not deceived by their agents. Aware of their surveillance.

The room is bugged, of course; a two-way system so they can whisper threats to him during the night.

When he leaves, Mrs. Fielding admits them into the room where they read his papers (he is smart enough to write in code), move things, tamper with his guns, poison his food.

There are so many of them, and he is alone.

Alone except for the great powers, the shadowy allies who counsel and aid him. He develops his occult genius: he can alter the past, exert control over the present, see into the future. He can, at will, separate his spirit from his body and roam freely through time and space.

He knows who they are.

He knows how to strike, and when.

And then one morning he gets out of bed, slowly dresses, packs the few items he will need, loads his guns, and goes down into the kitchen to see Mrs. Fielding.

Was that how it had been? I doubted that I would ever know.

I wanted a cigarette. "Do you smoke?" I asked the girl.

She turned to me. "No."

"Paul?"

"What?"

"Do you smoke?"

"What?"

"Do you smoke cigarettes?"

He shook his head. "Erich does," he said.

Where were all the brave fire-eating manhunters now? Perhaps stalking from tree to tree through the wooded slopes of the ski mountain, tasting bile and smelling their own fear-sweat. Snapping off shots at the wind and shadows and their comrades. And Ralph was here, miles away, laying siege to a stone hut which contained a friend, a pretty college girl, and a young man who wanted so desperately to be elsewhere that he had packed up and gone away in such a hurry that he'd left his body behind.

"Do you have a mirror?" I asked the girl.

"Pardon?"

"A mirror, a compact?"

"No." She paused, looking at me. "What do you want a mirror for?"

"With a mirror I could look out of the window without having my head blown off."

"Oh. I'm sorry, no."

Murphy was watching us.

"Are you okay?" I asked him.

"I'm cold," he said.

"So am I."

"Poor Paul," Karen Bright said.

"He'll be okay."

"Has he lost his mind?"

"No. A circuit was overloaded and a fuse has temporarily blown out."

"Are you a certified electrician?" she asked dryly.

"I mean that he wasn't able to cope with the stress. When the stress is removed he'll come around."

"He acts like a sulky little boy."

Murphy was watching us from the far side of the room; he did not seem to be disturbed by our comments.

"Two years ago," I said, "I stopped at the scene of an automobile accident. Several people had been killed. When I arrived, the two survivors, a man and a woman, strangers, were wandering around together. The man was saying that he was an insurance salesman, top-dollar man in the area, and that he had just renewed the medical and life policies on his wife and two kids. The woman had some facial cuts, and she wiped them with her palms and then looked down at the blood, and—I swear this is true—she said that that particular red would make a lovely color for the drapes in her house. They were carrying on two separate conversations. Their faces were pale, they were trembling, and their voices sounded something like a thirty-three-and-a-third record played at forty-five rpm's. Cocktail party chatter. They weren't lunatics or monsters. They were simply unable at that moment to accept what had happened. Their lives had been shattered, and they were escaping the horror and grief."

The girl was silent for a time, and then she said: "I suppose if Erich hadn't been so stubborn, none of this would have happened. We would all have been gone from here."

"'Mights' don't count for much," I said.

"The man who was with you. Frank?"

"Frank Treblene."

"Was he a good friend?"

"An old, good friend."

"I'm sorry. Erich—I had dated him a few times, I liked him, but I really didn't know him very well."

I did not speak.

"Oh, God," she said softly. "There must be something wrong with me. I can't feel anything, I really can't. This isn't sad or horrible or tragic—it's just stupid. Idiotic. You get up in the morning and everything is beautiful, and then men are killed, and we three may be dead soon, too, and it's all so stupid. If I live, I'll never be able to feel calm or secure again. How can you? The sun was shining and then it got dark, and I don't think the darkness will ever go away."

"You're in shock, too," I said. "It just hit you differently."

"Mister," Paul Murphy said.

I looked across the room. He was sitting with his back against the wall, his knees drawn up and enfolded by his arms.

"Mister, I have to go to the bathroom."

"This place doesn't have one."

"I can't go outside, you know that."

"Make do," I said.

"Karen?" he said.

"Do you have to urinate, Paul?"

"Yes."

"Go in the fireplace."

"The ashes," he said. "It will smell bad."

"That's all right, Paul."

"Karen," he said.

"I'll close my eyes."

"Promise?"

"Yes, Paul." She smiled faintly.

Murphy got up, staying away from the window, and urinated into the fireplace. The embers hissed and smoked. He was right; there was an unpleasant odor.

I thought that if one of the three of them had to be killed, then it was unfortunate that it hadn't been Murphy. He was a natural victim. Kemp would have been a valuable ally.

One would expect the time to pass very slowly. It did not; the afternoon vanished like a dream. The sun melted the frost off the south and west windows, and I could see splashes of the dark blue sky; the air coming in through the broken window above my head warmed slightly; a great mass of snow slid hissing off the roof and landed outside with an impact that rattled plates and utensils in the cupboards; the light changed, diminished.

I got up and crossed the room, staying below the windows, and sat next to Murphy. He was shivering from cold and fear.

"How is it going?" I asked him quietly.

"All right," he said in a breathy shuddering voice.

"Listen, Paul, he'll be coming for us soon. You'll have to help me."

"What can *I* do?"

"You'll have to improvise. When the action starts, you must react quickly."

"Maybe he's gone away."

"Maybe."

"I'm so stiff and cold," he said petulantly.

"We're all cold. Ralph Brace is cold, too."

"He'll kill me."

"He has a rifle, but he has to come in after us or stick the rifle in through a window. The three of us should be able to overpower him."

"Oh, God, I don't think"—he hesitated for an instant, his teeth chattering—"I can *do* it."

"You'll be okay once it starts. But you must help Karen and me."

"I'll try."

"Fine."

"But I can't think—I'm so *confused*. Oh, Jesus, I'm going to die here!"

"The only way to live is to fight."

"Yes, yes," he said.

"I'm going back over to the other window now. It's getting dark. He'll be coming for us soon."

Murphy buried his face in his palms.

ELEVEN

Dusk came as quickly and mysteriously as had the dawn. When I stood up I had the illusion that the light remaining in the room was being drawn outward through the still-glowing windows, swirling and streaming away like smoke toward air vents. I was acutely aware of the silence. I heard the blood pulsing in my ears. I turned my head and could hear the faint crepitation of my neck muscles. Murphy cocked his head and looked up at me. The girl was listening, too, her eyes wide, the fingertips of one hand lightly touching her mouth.

We listened. And it occurred to me that we really were not listening to the silence—it had been equally quiet much of the afternoon; we must have subliminally perceived a sound and were now exploring the silence to locate its source and meaning. We were not interested in the silence, then, but in what might have disturbed it. I felt, I *knew* that Ralph was close, as prey is sometimes aware that a predator is near without actually hearing, smelling or sighting it—through an uneasiness, a sense of being observed, messages received on so deep a level that they cannot be traced. If there is a sixth sense, it might be this primitive, wholly unconscious attunement to stealth; an inheritance from our ancestors of the caves and savannahs, the same thing that now prompts us to become uneasy and turn around when someone stares at us in a certain way, or follows us down several city streets.

We waited.

"Jack." Ralph's voice, coming from the broken window.

I hurried across the room and stood close to the wall. The broken window was a few feet to my left.

"Jack, I want all of you to come out of there now."

He was on the other side of the wall, perhaps directly opposite me.

"Jack?"

"We're staying here," I said.

"Open the door, goddamn you!"

"Huff and puff all you want, Ralph."

"I'm not going to hurt you people," he said. His voice was the same, a husky baritone without much inflection. He had a habit of half-smiling when he talked, and I could hear the smile in his voice now.

"You won't hurt us?"

"No, I promise."

"You can probably see Frank from where you're standing," I said.

"I'm sorry about Frank," he said.

"So am I, Ralph." I signaled to the girl and Murphy to move over against the east wall, out of the line of his fire if he moved to the window. They crawled hurriedly across the floor.

"Frank was aiming his rifle at me. He might just have been using the telescope, but how could I know that? I shot first, Jack, that's all."

"What about the others?"

"Jack, I'm running out of patience. Now, I broke into the storehouse this morning and took three cans of the explosive. Do you understand?"

There was a cinderblock building close to the upper tram terminal where the howitzer and its ammunition and the canisters of avalanche explosives were kept. Ralph could have broken in there easily enough; he might even still have his key.

"Jack, are you thinking about it? All I have to do is activate one of the cans and throw it in a window. Now, you can figure out what the concussion will be like for you inside those stone walls."

"How do I know you really have the cans?"

"You figure out the probability, Jack, but don't take too long. It's cold out here."

"You'll kill us anyway."

"If I intended to kill you, I'd just throw in one of the cans."

"What *are* your plans?"

"I'm going to use you folks as hostages. Who ever heard of dead hostages?"

"I don't believe you," I said.

"It's your choice," he said.

"Wait. Give me a second to talk to the others."

"Jack, I've been out in this snow and cold for ten hours. I'm cold, man, and I'm starting to get mad."

"Thirty seconds," I said.

Murphy and the girl were sitting close together at the juncture of the wall and floor. I approached them.

"Well," I said softly, "what do you think?"

"Does he really have explosives?" she asked.

"I'm pretty sure he does. He knows where they're kept, and he's used them before."

"Will he throw one in here?"

"Yes."

"Will he kill us if we go outside?"

"I don't know. He might really want to use us as hostages."

"What choice do we have?" she asked.

"I think we'd better do as he says."

"Yes. Maybe he won't hurt us."

"Murphy?"

He tried to speak and could not. He swallowed, his Adam's apple bobbing, and then he nodded.

I returned to the window. "Ralph, we're coming out."

"Throw your guns through the window, first."

"We don't have any guns."

"Jack, goddamn it now, I said—"

"We *don't!* Frank was the only one who was armed."

"How many people are in there?"

"Three."

"I hope you're not lying to me, Jack."

"Only three."

"I want you to wait about twenty seconds and then come through the door one at a time, spaced about ten feet apart. Got that? You first, Jack, with your hands high. Keep walking; get out in the open away from the cabin. Last one out close the door. All right."

I heard the whisper of the deep snow as he moved to a new position. I slowly counted to twenty, unbolted the door, swung it open, raised my hands and stepped through the door frame and into the trench. I walked up the icy ramp. I passed Frank's body, reached the thigh-deep snow and kept going.

"Okay, hold it there," Ralph said. "Don't turn around." He was behind me somewhere, probably around the corner of the building.

Here, outside in the snowy bowl of mountains, the light lingered and strengthened itself on all the reflecting surfaces, creating a cove of dusk in the ocean of night. The temperature had fallen ten or fifteen degrees since sunset. It was very cold, and it would get colder.

"What's your name, friend?" Ralph asked.

"Paul Murphy."

"Okay, Murph, move up there with my pal Jack."

Murphy came up and stood next to me. His breathing was shallow and rapid. He was sweating from fear, and his face as well as his breath steamed in the cold. I heard the door slam shut, and a moment later the girl joined us. We stood abreast, our hands in the air.

"Jack, if there's anyone still inside the cabin . . ."

"There isn't," I said.

"What's your name, honey?" A pause. "Girl, what is your name?"

"What?" Karen asked.

"I asked, what is your name?"

"Karen."

"Okay, Karen, now you turn around and walk over to me. No, keep your hands up. That's right. Come here, all the way. Now hold it. Don't jump like that, Karen; I'm just searching you for weapons. Stop flinching; you've been felt before, haven't you? Okay. Now, in a moment you're going down into the cabin ahead of me. Did you hear? Are you sleeping, honey? Hey! Did you hear me?"

"Yes. I heard. Yes."

"Jack."

"What?"

"Don't turn around. I want you and the Murph to lie face down in the snow. Spread-eagled, got that?"

"Okay."

"Don't tell me 'okay,' Jack; just do it."

Murphy and I sprawled out in the deep, cold snow. I turned my head to the side so that I could breathe.

Ralph approached and then I could feel his hands moving over my body, searching me. He took my pocketknife. He searched Murphy then.

"Jack, I'm going down into the cabin for a second. I'll be out of there quickly, and so you decide whether or not you want to get up while I'm gone. Okay, Karen, go on. Christ, honey, you just *have* to wake up."

"What?" she said. "What is it?"

"Go through the door and then walk into the center of the room and stand there."

"Yes," she said.

I heard the door open. The snow was very cold and was filtering through my clothing; my cheeks, neck, and wrists were beginning to numb.

Ralph returned. "Jack, you and your boy Murph get up and go inside the cabin. I'll be close behind. It's dark in there, and I don't want to misunderstand your intentions—move very slowly straight on back to the fireplace."

Murphy and I got up out of the snow, turned and walked toward the cabin. Ralph was off to the side, grinning, covering us with his rifle, but once we had passed he moved in behind us. We walked down the trench and through the open door. Karen was standing by the fireplace. We moved directly across the room and stood with her.

Ralph closed and bolted the door. "Cozy," he said.

"Ralph," I said, "let us go."

He ignored me. "Murph, light those kerosene lanterns on the table."

Murphy, moving jerkily, stepped forward and turned the valves on the two lanterns. His hands were trembling violently, and he had difficulty striking a match. He finally got one burning, but by then the wicks had been saturated with fuel and they ignited with soft, huffing explosions. Murphy burned his hand.

Ralph, watching us, leaned his rifle against the door, removed his rucksack and then picked up the rifle again.

"I don't see any of the canisters," I said.

He smiled. "Well, Jack, I don't have any."

"Jesus Christ," I said.

"I should have got some, but I didn't think about them until about an hour ago."

I said nothing.

"You were never that easy to bluff in poker, Jack."

"Three people wouldn't die if I guessed wrong in poker," I said.

Ralph moved toward the center of the room. His cheeks were red and slightly swollen from the cold. The blond stubble on his face glinted in the lantern glow. His hair was tousled from the pressure of his parka hood. There was not enough light to bring out the color of his eyes, but I remembered that they were blue, dark blue fading to a pale blue, almost silver, around the rims. Now the irises were enlarged to gather in the light. He looked like a college football player, a running back, or the model in a soft-drink advertisement.

"I suppose you're wondering why I gathered you here this evening," he drawled.

There was something of the actor in Ralph. It had always been there, but never so obviously as now. He possessed the actor's facility of playing his role with concentration and at the same time observing himself, evaluating his own performance and the performances of the other actors, sensing the audience's mood (Karen, Murphy and I were both actors and audience in his little improvisational drama), adjusting his timing. He was not a good actor. There was a slight exaggeration in all that he did: the lazily graceful way he moved, the wryly humorous expression with which he regarded us, the soft but authoritative drawl in his voice.

"Murph, why don't you throw a couple logs on that fire," he said.

Ralph was not at all what I had expected. He was insane, of course, but you could not say he was a maniac; that is, he was not wildly agitated or incoherent. His madness was far more tightly controlled than I had supposed.

"Karen, sweetie, put some water on one of those little stoves. I'll have some coffee, or cocoa if you have it. Do you have cocoa, Karen?"

"Hot chocolate," she said. "Yes."

"Jack—well, hell, let me see if I can think of some way for you to keep your hands busy."

He did not intend to hurt us, at least not right now. We were necessary to his drama. Ralph needed us, it seemed, in order to assure himself of his own importance and power and reality. The mountains had been an empty stage. Now he would be able to see himself reflected in us. We were to serve temporarily as his mirrors and echoes. He would define himself through our reactions to him. He could feed and grow on our fear; gratify himself on our total dependence; realize a godlike sense of omnipotence by exercising the power of death—giving it or withholding it. I thought he would kill us sooner or later.

TWELVE

Roof timbers creaked, the last light faded from the windows, the stone walls exhaled a new, acid cold. The long winter night was here; we had fourteen or fifteen hours until dawn.

Karen lit one of the Primus stoves and put a saucepan of water on the burner. She did not seem so desperately intense now; Ralph's smiling, lazy ways had relaxed her.

Murphy got three split juniper logs from the woodpile and placed them on the ashes in the fireplace.

"Put some kerosene on the logs," Ralph said.

"What?" Murphy asked.

"Jack, are those two people hard of hearing? Do they want me to pass them notes?"

"Paul," I said, "there's a two-gallon can of kerosene in one of the cupboards. Get it and pour some on the logs."

Murphy, still moving jerkily, went around the table and down the east wall toward the row of cupboards.

"Jack, are you going to have to translate for me all night?"

"He's scared," I said.

"The fox, too?"

"Yes."

"Are you scared, Jack?"

"Yeah."

He smiled. "But you seem to hear what I say."

"I'm concentrating, Ralph."

Murphy returned with the can of kerosene. He didn't seem to know what came next.

"Pour some on the logs," I said.

"Now be careful, Murph," Ralph said. "There might be some live coals beneath that ash. You've burned your hand once already."

"Go ahead, Paul," I said.

He splashed a pint or so of kerosene over the logs and then straightened.

"A little more," I said.

He leaned over. Kerosene gushed from the spout.

"That's enough!" I said.

He straightened again, watching me.

"The kid's retarded, Jack."

"I told you, he's scared."

"Jack, this boy is stupid."

"He's waiting for another order," I said.

"Oh, hell—light the fire, will you, Jack?"

I got a book of matches from my pocket, struck one and tossed it onto the kerosene-saturated logs; there was a snapping noise, then a humming, and for a moment the flames escaped the fireplace and curled up over the mantel.

"The water is boiling now," Karen said.

"Jack, does she require explicit instructions?"

"I guess."

"Would you convey my wish to the lady?"

"Make him the cup of hot chocolate, Karen," I said.

"How are you doing, Murphy?"

"What?" And then quickly, "Fine, sir."

"Now, Murph, I have a task for you. Are you listening? I want you to close off the broken window. I don't care how you do it, or with what materials; I just want you to prevent the cold air from blowing in. Do you understand, son? Use a little of that good old American ingenuity. Don't ask me any questions, don't wait for instructions, just do it."

"But—"

"No!"

"But I don't—"

"Murphy!" I said. "Wake up. There should be some plyboard sheets in one of the cabinets, and some nails and a hammer, too. Block the window. Don't talk."

Murphy slowly moved away.

"I don't like that kid," Ralph said.

"The hot chocolate is ready," Karen said.

"Carry it over here and set it down on the table. That's right. Okay, go back to where you were."

Murphy had found some materials, and now he moved behind Ralph, toward the broken window.

"Murph," Ralph said without turning, "I like to hear a man whistle while he works. I want you to start whistling now and keep whistling until you move out from behind my back. Do you understand?"

"Yes."

"Whistle," Ralph said, smiling at me.

Murphy began to whistle.

"I don't know," Ralph said. "This just isn't working."

Murphy was whistling "Waltzing Matilda."

"I've got a man behind me, a cup of hot cocoa cooling on the table, and this rifle. You people have the warmth of the fire. I can't get warm, I can't drink my cocoa—Jack, you're waiting for the chance to try me, aren't you?"

"No."

"Of course you are. I know you. All I have to do is relax for a second and you'll be all over me. You aren't like that lamb over there—you intend to wait for an opportunity and then take it. Well, okay. I'd do the same."

I did not speak.

"That Murph can really whistle," Ralph said.

"He's a musician," Karen said.

"Karen, honey, you're so pretty, so sweet, and then you have to talk and ruin everything. Jack, this just isn't working. My cocoa has stopped steaming. I'm cold, and I'm losing my temper. I'm the homicidal maniac here"—he grinned—"and I believe that on that basis alone I should occupy a position of comfort and honor. I want to be next to the fire, folks. Okay, Jack, you and the little fox move around the table to the left—no, *your* left—while I go around this side. *Slowly*, Jack; you can get hurt moving so fast. All right. Ah, it's warm here. Karen, slide my cold cocoa down to this end of the table. Don't pick up the cup, just slide it. Leave it there. Now go back and stand with my pal Jack. Fine. And now slide one of the benches down to your end of the table. No, Jack, stay where you are; let the fox do it. Okay. Look, the bench isn't that heavy; just drag it around. Yes. Oh, I'm proud of you. Sit down, both of you. Right. Listen to the Murph. Murphy, you can stop whistling now. He sounds like a teakettle."

Murphy, at the far end of the room, cut his whistle off in mid-note.

"This is still awkward," Ralph said. "There is scum on my cocoa. No, this won't do at all. Karen is a sweetie-pie, and the whistler couldn't hurt a fly, but you, Jack, you're a bad ass, and I don't trust you at all. Jack, I like you, but you've got a mean streak."

He cradled the rifle against his right side, his finger on the trigger, the muzzle directed toward my chest, and then slowly, with his left hand, he unzipped his coat.

"No homicidal maniac worthy of the title has only one weapon," he said.

He reached across his body with his left hand, lifted the jacket flap, and withdrew a pistol from the holster. It looked like a Luger or a Walther PPK 38. He released the safety and then moved crabwise to the corner, watching us, and leaned the rifle against the wall.

"Now," he said.

He shifted the pistol to his right hand and, with his left, dragged the other bench around to his end of the table.

"Right," he said.

He sat down. The table was about ten feet long; he sat at the fire end, Karen and I across from him. The lanterns, one at each end of the table, glowed brightly. The Primus stove still burned with a hissing noise. Ralph reached out with his left hand, picked up the cup of cocoa, and tasted it.

"Aw, Christ," he said. "It's almost ice cream."

"I'll heat it," Karen said.

"Do that, honey."

She rose from the bench, moved around the table, took the cup and the stove, and carried them to our end of the table. She poured the cocoa back into the saucepan and placed it on the burner.

"Mister," Murphy said.

"What?"

"I sealed the window."

"You did? Did you hear? The Murph closed off the broken window. Murph, my man, by Jesus, this will not go unnoticed in Washington. Come over here and sit with your comrades. Goofy son of a bitch. Sit down there. Well, this *is* cozy."

The fire burned behind him; I could not clearly see his face. He rested his right forearm on the table. The pistol was aimed at me; he did not fear Murphy or the girl.

"Murph, what do you do?"

"Pardon?"

"What do you *do*, lad?"

"Oh. I'm a student."

"That is precisely as it should be. Where?"

"At the University. Of Colorado. Boulder."

"Murph, I've learned all about you that I care to know. Karen? Don't say 'what,' Karen."

"I'm a student, too," she said.

"That's enough," he said. "Jack, what do you do?"

I did not reply.

"Jack?"

I remained silent.

"Jack."

"You know what I do, Ralph." I thought the girl and Murphy were too passive, too eager to please him; it was a mistake to nourish his sense of power.

"Jack." He raised the pistol slightly, so that the muzzle was aimed between my eyes.

I looked at him. I might have done anything to live. If falling to my knees had been the expedient act at that moment, I probably would have done it; but I felt certain that Ralph was not ready to kill me now. I was the only person in the room who had known him before—he needed me.

"Is the cocoa ready?" he asked.

"I think so," Karen said. "Yes."

"Bring it down here. Throw it in my face if you think Jack is fast."

The hot liquid steamed in the cool of the room. He blew on the surface, sipped it, set the cup back down on the table.

"Jack, I suppose I caused quite a fuss down in town."

"Fuss is hardly the word."

"Cops all over the place?"

"Cops, citizens, the National Guard, the—"

"The National Guard?" He seemed amused.

"They were supposed to bring in some helicopter gun ships."

"I'm big game," he said wryly.

"Did you hear or see any helicopters?" I asked him.

"No. So this is a pretty big thing, Jack?"

"Very big."

"Are there any reporters around?"

"The town is filled with journalists, and more coming in all the time."

"Television people, too?"

"Yes, quite a few."

"Did I make the network news last night?"

"All three networks."

"Jesus," he said, smiling. There was something boyishly enthusiastic about him now, and for some reason that made him seem all the more obscenely dangerous.

He sipped his cocoa. "What did they say about me?"

"I don't think they'd had time to dig up too much before air time—just your age, general background, part of your police record."

"Did they show a photograph of me? I left some pictures in my room."

"I didn't see the news, Ralph. Jan told me about it."

"How is Jan?"

"Fine."

"And your kids?"

"Just fine, Ralph." I could feel the hair rising on my arms and the back of my neck.

"Did Walter Cronkite himself report my story?"

"I don't know. Probably not—most likely it was reported by the Denver CBS affiliate."

"I suppose I'll be on the front page of the newspapers tonight and tomorrow."

"Every daily in the country."

"Do you think I'll be on the television news tonight again?"

"Absolutely."

"Did they say that I'm insane?"

"I don't know. That seems to be the general opinion."

This seemed to puzzle him. "Did the newspapers print my journal? Didn't the television reporters mention it?"

"Not that I know of."

"I left it in my room, with the photographs."

"I'm sure the cops have it. Maybe they just haven't released it to the press."

"I explained everything in my journal."

"I'm sure it will be released eventually."

"All of this has been for *nothing* if the information in my journal isn't disseminated." He sipped the cocoa. He appeared gloomy now, almost sullen.

"What did you write in your journal, Ralph?"

"Never mind."

"Your journal is probably being read on television right at this moment."

"Do you think so?"

"I'm sure of it."

"Okay. Listen, Jack, I want you to do something."

I listened.

"I want you to go outside and get our ski equipment."

"All right."

"The skis and poles for the four of us here."

"Then you are going to use us as hostages?"

"That's right."

"I'll get the things," I said, rising.

"Take off your boots and stockings, Jack."

"What?"

"Don't say 'what,' Jack—just take off your boots and stockings."

I sat on the bench and began unlacing my boots.

"If you want to run, Jack, go ahead."

I pulled off my right boot.

"I won't stop you."

"I won't be going anywhere barefoot," I said.

"I know."

I removed my left boot and the gaiter, then pulled off the long woolen knicker stocking and the cotton stocking beneath it.

"Where did you leave your car?" he asked.

"On the old jeep road."

"Do you have the keys?"

"It's Frank's jeep. The keys are in his pocket."

"Get them."

My legs were bare to just below the knees now.

"The moon will rise above the ridge somewhere around nine thirty tonight," Ralph said. "We'll ski down then."

I nodded.

"Bring in the skis and we'll wax up."

"Okay."

"And the keys to Frank's jeep."

I stood up. "Is it all right if I go now?"

"Sure, Jack."

"I'll take one of the lanterns."

"There's a flashlight in the side pocket of my rucksack. Take that."

THIRTEEN

Long streamers of mist, like jet contrails, were strung out across the night sky. One serpentine cloud, captured by local winds, had turned back upon itself and was slowly beginning to coil around the summit of the Wolf. In the clear areas between the long, wind-ripped clouds, the speckled glow of the Milky Way vibrated against the dimensionless blue-black night.

I waded through the snow. My feet and lower legs ached with the cold. Snow crystals sparkled in the flash-light beam, burst into a cold white fire.

I found Frank's rifle. Ralph had removed the bolt. I had hoped . . .

Frank's body was half-buried in the snow. There was a ragged-looking hole about the size of a quarter above his left eye, and half of the back of his head had been blown away. His features—eyes, nose, mouth, jawline—were intact, but it was not Frank anymore: the body seemed to have the same relation to Frank as firewood has to a tree. You can look at a log, feel the texture of the bark, count the age rings, determine that it came from a certain type and size of tree, and even try to picture that particular tree in your mind; but there is no way of pretending that the log is the tree. That is the way it was with Frank; more of him was missing than a little bone and tissue and brain. I understood now why undertakers call a corpse the "remains." Frank Treblene was gone. All that was left was the sack of chemicals that had contained him.

The corpse was frozen; when I levered an arm, the entire body moved. I unbuckled the straps of his rucksack, removed it and set it aside. I went through his pockets until I found his cigarettes and a package of matches and the keys to his jeep.

My legs were numbing.

I felt alone on a frozen, dead planet, but then I heard the ventriloquistic *yip-yip* howling of some coyotes. They were far away, perhaps below in the forest, but the sound carried and echoed, and I felt surrounded by their half-mournful, half-comical lunatic chorus. One coyote sounded like five; five like twenty-five; and twenty-five would probably sound like the hounds of hell.

I could not feel my feet. The exposed skin of my face was numbing, too. The air was sharp in my lungs. I estimated the temperature to be about thirty degrees below zero, but it might have been colder. It would certainly reach forty below, possibly fifty below, in the coldest hours preceding dawn, unless the new low pressure area arrived first. The storm would carry warm air, and more snow.

Erich Kemp had been shot in the chest. There was a large amount of still-red blood on the snow; perhaps the cold and the moistness of the snow had preserved some of the color. Kemp had dug up the skiing equipment before he died; three pairs of skis and poles leaned against the stone cabin wall. I carried Murphy's and Karen's ski equipment around the corner and stuck them into the snow near the trench. I found Ralph's outfit on the east side of the cabin; he was using regular alpine skis.

I could flex my knees, but below them my legs were completely dead. The simple act of walking required concentration. I carried two sets of skis and poles inside the cabin and then went back outside for the other two sets.

Ralph, a dark figure against the shuddering red glow of the fire, said, "Is it cold out there, Jacky?"

Shadows contracted and expanded over the walls and ceiling. I stacked the skis and poles in the corner and then walked stiffly, flat-footed, to the table.

"Did you find Frank's rifle?" Ralph asked.

I sat down on the end of the bench. "No."

He laughed.

My feet and lower legs were hard and had turned a grayish white color; blood had retreated from the surface of the skin, and the small capillaries had closed. I removed my mittens and began rubbing my right foot.

"You had a chance to escape, Jack," Ralph said.

"Sure."

He still held the pistol, but he was not aiming it at me. He appeared comfortable and relaxed.

The fire hissed and crackled, shooting streams of sparks up the chimney. The heat penetrated about halfway into the cabin now; I could feel it. I rubbed my right foot and leg until they began to prickle and ache, and then I switched to my left leg. Another few minutes' walking through the snow, in that terrible cold, and my feet might have been seriously frostbitten.

Murphy, next to me, sat with his head bowed and his hands folded on the table. He seemed half-asleep.

"Would you like more hot chocolate?" Karen asked.

"No," Ralph said. "I'm hungry, though. What have you got to eat?"

"Well, salami, cheese, rye bread, some dehydrated soup, and wine—we have a bottle of red wine."

"You have wine?"

"We were going to drink it for lunch, and then . . ."

"Open the wine and bring it to me," Ralph said. "And then make a couple of sandwiches and boil some soup. How much food do you have?"

"Quite a lot."

"Then you folks shall be my dinner guests."

Karen got the bottle of wine and a corkscrew from a rucksack.

I wished she had not mentioned the wine; there was no telling how the alcohol might affect Ralph.

Sensation began returning to my left foot; I kept massaging the skin until it too began to prickle and burn. My boots were on the floor and where I had left them, but the stockings were gone.

"I warmed up your socks for you, Jack," Ralph said. He leaned down and got my two pairs of stockings from the fireplace ledge and tossed them to me.

"Thanks," I said.

"What are pals for?"

The wool was smoking from the heat. The stockings felt good against my still-cold skin.

Karen opened the bottle, slid it down to the other end of the table, then returned and got the bread, cheese, and salami from her rucksack.

"I don't have a knife," she said.

Ralph reached into his pocket with his left hand, withdrew a knife—the one he had taken from me—and tossed it to her. He poured some wine into the same cup he had used for the hot chocolate. The wine scared me: he probably had not eaten for many hours, he was fatigued, and it was a full bottle—enough to get him fairly drunk.

Karen was slicing the cheese. Murphy had not moved.

"How are your legs, Jack?"

"They hurt."

"Will you be able to ski down?"

I nodded.

"That's the spirit." He drank some of the wine.

"What are you going to do with us, Ralph?"

"Take you to Mexico. You'd like to go to Mexico, wouldn't you? Warm and sunny there."

"We'd never get through the roadblocks."

"That's what hostages are for, Jack." He sipped his wine.

"Ralph," I said, "aren't you going to share the wine with us?"

"No. Don't abuse my hospitality by asking."

I tried to wiggle my toes; they were a little stiff yet, but I could move them.

"Karen, honey, just cheese for me. I don't eat meat."

I looked up at him. "Are you a vegetarian now, Ralph?"

"That's right. I don't eat dead animals."

"But you're drinking alcohol."

"Jesus drank wine."

"Didn't Jesus eat meat?"

"No. No holy man eats meat, Jack."

"What is your journal about?" I asked.

"It's very complex."

"I'd like to hear about it."

"Jack, don't patronize me."

"I'm not. I really would like to know."

"It took me a year—hell, a lifetime—to refine the ideas I've put down in that notebook. It's important, damned important." He finished his wine and poured more into the cup. He did everything left-handed; his right hand gripped the pistol.

"Jack, I've put it all together. I've synthesized the whole of human knowledge and united it to the mysteries. My work is partly original and partly a unification. What I've done, briefly, is to fuse the spiritual to the physical. I've united science and religion, the body and the soul, the brain and the heart. Think of the sum of human knowledge as a chain, but one with as many links missing as extant—the unknown, the mysteries, are the missing links. Do you see? What I've done is to link the chain into a single, integral whole. You can see how profoundly important that is."

"Yes," I said. The cracks in Ralph's psyche were starting to show.

"Ralph," I asked, "are the killings related to your synthesis?"

"Of course. They are an exercise in metaphysical will. Crystal moments of existential awareness."

I nodded slowly.

"Are you bothered by my . . . my *crimes?*" he asked, ironically accenting the word "crimes."

"Yes," I said.

"Why, Jack?"

Karen relit the Primus stove and put a pan of water on the burner. Murphy had lifted his head; he was listening now.

"Well," I said, "because murder is wrong."

"How do you know it is?" He was smiling faintly.

"You talked about human knowledge before. Isn't it a fact that we've been taught, for thousands of years, that killing another human being is wrong?"

"Yes, and what is the result of that absurd concept? For thousands of years—maybe for hundreds of thousands of years—we've been waging war, killing, slaughtering. Contrast the doctrine of the liar prophets with the actuality. What is right, *is.* It's stupid to yearn for the unreal, the *not is.* Killing and being killed are not only entirely natural but entirely necessary—in the same way a forest fire is necessary to ensure the future health and growth of the forest. You're a forester, Jack; you know that in the long run forest fires are beneficial."

"I can't buy your analogy," I said. "Killing *is* wrong."

He poured more wine into his cup. "Jack, like most people, especially those in Western society, you're hung up on the primitive judgmental plane. Listen to me: there is no right or wrong, good or bad, past or future, life or death; there is only the essential Oneness and the Now."

I stared at him. "I don't understand."

He smiled indulgently, as a teacher might smile at a student who, though he tries very hard, is not quite bright enough to grasp the significance of a transparently simple concept. I knew I had made a mistake in inquiring about his "ideas."

"Well, it's almost time to eat," I said. "Let's get back to this later."

"Jack, you're disturbed by what this society calls death, right? But death is only a different dimension of awareness. You might say that I chose, or was chosen, to kill those people, but the truth is they have just been liberated from an inferior mode of existence. Now, I have to use these words, your vocabulary, but try to remember that there is neither existence nor nonexistence, but only an orderly progression of various spiritual-material states, culminating in the final submergence of the particular into the All." His diction had improved; he spoke precisely, almost pedantically now. The more irrational he became, the more carefully he selected his words.

"You seem to have thought about this a lot, Ralph."

He nodded.

I could see that he was enjoying this "intellectual" discussion and that he would not become angry if I disagreed with him. In fact, disagreement was expected of me.

"Ralph," I said, "you aren't making any sense at all."

"Do you think I'm crazy?" he asked.

I hesitated. "Yes," I said.

"Jack, I am one of the few completely sane men on this planet. What you second-phase carnates call insanity is really just the holy state of inner-outer knowledge preliminary to the third release. Those people you say I killed? They killed themselves, Jack. They, I—we are the same. I love them. I was the energy-love they chose for release. They'll reappear as something else, somewhere else."

"Are you talking about reincarnation?" I asked.

"That's not the best word for it, but okay."

"What is this release you talk about?"

"There are five releases, each higher than the last. The fifth and final release is the achievement of diffusion, being *everywhere,* seeing all, hearing all, knowing all, feeling nothing."

I glanced at Murphy and the girl. They were listening intently and seemed only slightly puzzled. They were young, and their generation was familiar with this sort of mystical gobbledygook.

I turned back to Ralph. "Your diffusion—you're talking about becoming a god?"

"The word 'god' is wholly inadequate. The concept of 'god' is a poor second-phase guess at a fifth-phase phenomenon."

"Are you a god now?" I asked.

"Only in the sense that, say, the Dalai Lama is a god. He is the living Buddha, but still a prisoner of spatial and temporal limitations."

"There is space and time, then?"

"There is the *illusion* of space and time."

"And the Dalai Lama is a prisoner of an illusion?"

"Yes. So were Jesus, Mohammed, Indra, and many others. This may surprise you, Jack, but I am a spiritual brother of the Dalai Lama."

"That does surprise me."

"You see my ears, how they sort of stick out? That's one of the signs, you know. And I have moles on my sides, the last vestige of the arms that used to grow out of my previous Buddha substance. It may be, Jack—I don't claim it, but there is evidence to support my feeling—it may be that I am the *true* Dalai Lama, and a terrible mistake was made in recognition. That could explain why China was able to seize Tibet, because a mistake was made in the recognition of the true Dalai Lama."

"Ralph, Buddhism forbids the killing of any creature. And yet you've killed many people in the last two days."

"You're still speaking of killing," he said. "Jack, haven't you been listening at all?"

"Maybe we should eat now," I said. "The food is ready."

"It can wait."

"I'm beginning to see it now," I said. "What we think of as death is merely the entrance into another phase of being."

"Exactly. It's impossible to *destroy* life. Life is energy, Jack, and energy is matter, and matter is energy. Neither energy nor matter can be destroyed, but only transformed from one back into the other, forever. It's just as Newton taught us."

"Wait," I said. "I thought that was Einstein, not Newton."

"They are the same persona in different material bodies," he said impatiently. "Euclid, Newton, Einstein—Jack, I had always thought you were an intelligent man."

"You've progressed far beyond mere intelligence, Ralph," I said.

He did not detect my irony, he was flattered.

"I am to you," he said, "as you are to a dog."

"Mister," Murphy said suddenly.

Ralph looked at him.

"I believe in reincarnation."

Ralph stared at Murphy for another moment and then turned to me, smiling. "Jack, I am to you as you are to a dog. And you are to Murphy as a dog is to a beetle."

"What are flying saucers, Ralph?"

He shrugged. "A conveyance."

"The Bermuda Triangle?"

"A pocket of fifth-phase space on a second-phase planet."

"What really is the thing we call magic or sorcery or witchcraft?"

"The result of a successful petition to fifth-state beings to temporarily suspend the illusion of mechanistic cause and effect." He seemed slightly bored now with my stupidity. He did not want just to repeat his weird catechism; he wished to be challenged.

"Well, I'm starving," I said.

He poured the last of the wine into his cup. "I have enemies, Jack," he said quietly.

Oh, Christ, I thought; here it comes now.

"People who turned my eyes around, put hair in the milk, entered my mirror, put static on the radio." He spoke these senseless phrases with a casual drawling conviction, with no more emphasis than if he'd been discussing the football scores, but his eyes were wide and hard-looking.

"It wasn't me, Ralph," I said. "You know that."

"Denials are confirmation," he said, staring at me. "Affirmation is a denial. Silence is the offal of the unconvictioned."

"Ralph?"

"Do you think I'm joking?"

"Ralph," I said desperately, "if you are the Dalai Lama, then who is the Dalai Lama?"

"Insolent son of a bitch," he said. He was smiling, but not in a pleasant way. His body was still relaxed except for his right hand; I could see that his knuckles had whitened with the pressure of squeezing the gun handle.

"Ralph," Karen said lightly, trying to help me, "don't you think—"

"I can see your hair growing," Ralph said to me.

"—it's time to eat? The soup is—"

"The hair is growing down into your brain."

"—cold and I just thought . . ." Karen was smiling brightly, artificially.

"Millions of hairs growing down into your brain like worms."

"Won't you please join us for dinner?" Karen asked, her voice now lilting and crooning, as if she were talking to an infant.

He glanced at Karen, unaccountably charmed by her hysterical cheerfulness, and his tension drained away.

"Well, the hair cancer is your problem, Jack. Is there any pain?"

"Yes." Affirmation is denial.

"Jack, I want you to look at the Murph. See no evil, hear no evil, speak no evil, all rolled up into one evil stinking putty-fleshed bag of scum."

Murphy tried to smile and failed.

Ralph laughed. He shook his head. "Old Murph," he said tenderly. "You aren't happy here, are you, boy?"

As Karen had diverted Ralph to save me, I tried to divert him to help Murphy.

"Ralph," I said, "do you remember that time when we—"

"Poor old Murph. You were a camel before, and there is still too much camel in you now. You've got a hump in your back and a long camel neck and dumb camel eyes, and you chew lies with a lateral camel-grinding of your jaws." This was spoken in a kind of chant.

"Ralph," I said, "I can hardly remember a colder night."

He looked at me. “The hair worms are eating your brain, Jack. Does it hurt?”

“Yes.” Affirmation is denial.

“They’re growing down behind your eyes. Can you see them?”

“No.” Denial is confirmation.

“I’m so hungry I could eat a litter of baby skunks,” Ralph said cheerfully.

FOURTEEN

Ralph remained cheerful until he was halfway through the meal, and then he began complaining about the food: the soup was not hot enough, the bread was stale, the Swiss cheese was rubbery . . . wasn't there any more wine? His expression and voice became sulky, petulant. No mustard? Is there any coffee? No, I *hate* instant coffee.

He became silent. He frowned at me. The girl, Murphy, and I sat tensely, not moving, not looking at him.

"Turn off the goddamned radio," he said, and then he was silent for a long time.

"The moon should rise above the ridge soon," I said quietly.

The logs in the fireplace glowed a bright orange-red.

"Maybe we should wax up the skis now, Ralph."

He watched me suspiciously.

"It's cold," I said, "but we should have a fine ski run down in the moonlight."

I feared his silence, his paranoidal brooding over God knew what imaginary offenses and conspiracies. He had seemed to function fairly well on a practical level.

"Good powder snow," I said. "Ralph, remember that time when . . ."

He got up from the table, shifted the pistol to his left hand and moved sideways toward the woodpile. He was only five or six feet from me now. I waited for a chance. He glanced quickly at the woodpile, looked at me, glanced again at the woodpile, and then, watching me, bent down sideways and chose a stick of piñon from the pile. It was a branch, maybe eighteen inches long and four inches in diameter. I thought, if he turns when he throw it into the fire. . . . One side of his face glowed with reflected firelight; the other side was obscured by shadow. He was very fast: he suddenly lunged toward me, raising the club, and I did not have time to raise my arms. The club struck me on the long thick muscle where the curve of the neck merges into the shoulder, the same place a policeman will hit you with his nightstick if he elects not to break your head. I went backward over the bench, hit the floor, and scrambled on my hands and knees to the center of the room. Slowly I regained full awareness. There was no pain at first; the whole upper right side of my body was numbed.

The others were speaking. I could not comprehend their words. Ralph was shouting loudly, commanding; Murphy and the girl spoke softly, pleading, agreeing, whining.

I sat up. There was firelight on the ceiling, the walls. Ralph, Murphy, and Karen were still talking, but it sounded like a foreign language to me; there were syllables, words, sentences, but I could understand none of it.

And then the pain came. It ran in a line from my neck over the curve of my shoulder, down my arm to my fingertips. My fingers seemed to buzz. The pain increased wave by wave. I was both shivering and sweating. The pain reached a point where I could not tolerate any more, and then it got worse. My vision was affected; I had a kind of blurry, fish-eye lens's view of the cabin. And then gradually, wave by wave, the pain diminished.

"Get up," Ralph said.

I tried to get up, fell back; more pain. The right side of my body seemed paralyzed. I tried again, using my left arm, and it worked. I was standing.

Ralph was standing behind the table. He was surrounded by a trembling orange glow, and the lanterns on the table lit his face from below.

"You two," he said, "go back and stand with my old pal Jacky."

Murphy and the girl backed up until they stood with me.

"Well," Ralph said.

I was nauseated and sweating.

"It was a nice try," Ralph said. "But I tuned into the same frequency you were using. Good try, though."

I lifted my left hand, unsnapped my jacket and felt along the hard ridge of my collarbone. I could not feel a break.

"Please," Karen said. "Please don't hurt us."

In the fire and lantern glow, her hair was a reddish-gold aura around the perfect cameo of her profile.

Ralph paced back and forth beyond the table. He was excited now, triumphant. He paced, his eyes reflecting the lantern light; he grinned.

Murphy was making noises at the back of his throat. He paused to inhale, and then the noises continued. He hummed, groaned softly, hummed again.

Ralph laid his pistol on the table and then went to the corner for the rifle. We were about twenty feet away from him now; the rifle would be more accurate at that range.

"Please," the girl said. "*Why are you doing this to us?*"

Ralph slowly raised his rifle and aimed it at Murphy.

Murphy choked, said, "Aw, no. God, mister . . . aw, no . . ."

"You," Ralph said, "You . . . *camel!*"

"What?" Murphy said. "I didn't do any—what?"

"Shut up, Paul," I said.

You could not appease Ralph now; he was ignited by our fear, stimulated by our obedience. I did not believe he would kill us until after he had reduced us to things. He would kill us after he'd exercised his power, enjoyed his sport.

Ralph lowered his rifle and resumed pacing back and forth across the width of the room. His face appeared veined, blood-gorged in the lantern light.

He stopped. "You," he said to Murphy. "You, get down on your knees."

"Oh, please," Murphy said.

"Get down! Pray, you filthy camel!"

Murphy's body, all joints it seemed, suddenly collapsed, and his knees thumped heavily on the floor. He fell over onto his face, but then he quickly straightened and assumed an attitude of prayer. His eyes were closed. He raised his tear-glossed face toward the ceiling. His palms were joined beneath his chin. "Oh, please dear God, please oh my God oh no, don't, I'm so sorry, hurt me, I didn't mean oh please . . ."

Ralph laughed. "That's *good!*" he said.

"Oh, my God, if You'll only please—"

"To me!" Ralph said, pacing again. "Pray to me!"

Murphy's lips writhed, but no sound emerged.

"Pray!"

"Mister, mister, please help me I'm so sorry if you will only please . . ." His voice went hoarse, then silent, but his lips continued to move.

Ralph swung his rifle toward the girl. "You, take off your clothes."

"What?" she said. "Please, please, please."

He aimed through the telescopic sight.

Karen moved sideways until our arms touched. She looked up at me; her eyes were round, and there was a tic pulling at the corner of her mouth. She seemed vague, sleepy.

Murphy, kneeling on the floor, his face lowered onto the upper edges of his locked palms, was softly muttering and crying, and praying again to his god Ralph.

"You," Ralph said.

"Her name is Karen," I said.

"You, take off your clothes!"

"Ralph," I said, "her name is Karen. My name is Jack. The man on the floor is named Paul. We're *people,* Ralph, for God's sake!"

"You," he said again.

The girl was whimpering. The tic was pulling violently at the corner of her mouth, and another tic had started on the lid of her left eye. She found my hand with hers, clasped it. Her hand was small and very cold.

"Bitch whore slut, take off your clothes."

Karen Bright pulled her hand from mine and began undressing. She removed her jacket, her sweater, a turtleneck jersey, her bra. She was crying. She moved slowly, with the shaky coordination of a very small child. Weeping, she bent over and unzipped her gaiters, unlaced and removed her boots, then pulled down her ski pants. When the pants were around her ankles she slipped and fell on the floor. She finished removing her ski pants and then, without rising, pulled off her long underwear bottoms. She sat on the floor and wept quietly.

"You," Ralph said. "Stand up."

Her motor control seemed gone; she moved her arms and legs, strained, but was unable to rise. I reached down and lifted her to her feet. She wavered, almost fell, but then managed to remain erect with my partial support.

Ralph stared at her. It was not a look of lust, or of appreciation; he was smug, contemptuous, silently laughing.

"You," Ralph said to Murphy. "Now you take off your clothes."

Murphy muttered, prayed—he was all alone now.

"Wake him up," Ralph told me.

I stepped forward and kicked Murphy lightly on his back. He sobbed.

"Wake him up," Ralph said.

I kicked Murphy again.

Murphy slowly lifted his head. "What? What?"

"Take off your clothes," Ralph said.

"Pardon, sir?"

"Take-off-your-clothes!"

Murphy slowly began undressing.

The girl was shivering. I could feel the pimpled flesh on her upper arm, where I held her, and I could hear the light chattering of her teeth.

Murphy and Karen Bright were finished. Ralph had established his dominance; he had, in a real way, hypnotized them. They had surrendered their minds and bodies to him, and if he'd asked they probably would have cut their own throats. He owned them. They were not individuals anymore; they had become extended fragments of Ralph's will, his tools. I could feel my own self going, too, leaking out of me like water out of a cracked basin. I wanted to sleep, too. It would be so easy to surrender completely and die in a foggy dream. I hoped I would be able to recognize that last instant when I still retained the power of choice, so that I could at least avert the final horror of collaborating with my murderer. When the time came I wanted to run, shouting defiantly, into the muzzle of his rifle.

Murphy had undressed now. He looked up at Ralph and waited for his next command.

"Lie down on the floor," Ralph said to the girl.

"No," I said.

She pulled away from me, knelt, and then lay prone on the floor.

Ralph laughed. "No," he said. "Stupid bitch. On your *back.*"

She turned over and stared up at the ceiling.

"Spread your legs."

She did.

"Lift your knees."

She did.

"Get on top of her," Ralph said to Murphy.

"What?"

"Get on top of her."

"But—I don't know—"

"Didn't you hear me?" A low threatening tone, but Ralph was smiling.

Murphy crawled over and mounted the girl. He lifted his head and looked up at Ralph.

"Go ahead," Ralph said.

"But I can't," Murphy said.

"Fuck her."

"But I *can't.*"

"Fake it."

"What?"

"Pretend."

Murphy began making the motions of copulation.

Karen closed her eyes.

This was the entertainment of a totally impotent man. This was the measure of Ralph's disease: sex, the expression of the life force, and hatred, death's favorite emissary, had somehow been blended together in him and become a whole new thing, as several distinct metals combined under heat and pressure become an alloy.

I sensed Ralph's intent. I tensed, waited.

Ralph laughed. "Jack, Jack, look at that," he said. He moved out from behind the table. "Oh, Jack, look at them." He called me by name; he invited me to share his mirth.

And then he raised the rifle and shot Murphy through the head.

I rushed him then. He did not have enough time to work the rifle's bolt. I hit him full force with my left shoulder. He slammed back against the stone wall, and then we both fell to the floor.

He lost the rifle. I regained my feet first picked up the rifle by the barrel and swung it like a baseball bat. He was just rising to his knees, and the stock caught him behind the ear. He went down, out. I could hear the girl screaming. I stood there then, waiting, not knowing what came next. Ralph was unconscious. The girl screamed. I picked up the rifle, jammed the bolt home and aimed down at Ralph. I slowly applied pressure to the trigger—now!

I couldn't do it.

FIFTEEN

The girl had crawled half a dozen feet away from the body. She was crouched naked on the hardwood floor, her thighs drawn up against her breasts, her fists covering her eyes. She screamed and she screamed and she screamed.

The bullet had entered Murphy's head just above his ear. His wire-frame eyeglasses had not been damaged. There were brain and bone fragments and blood on the floor behind him.

Karen screamed, inhaled with a ripping sound, screamed.

Ralph was stirring on the floor now, moving his limbs, groaning.

I knelt on the floor alongside Karen. "It's okay now," I said.

Her fists covered her eyes.

She sobbed deeply, could not catch her breath for a moment, finally did, and screamed again.

I lightly touched her hair. "Karen, it's over."

She felt the pressure of my hand and suddenly recoiled, lifting her hands as if to ward off a blow. Her eyes, thickly lensed with tears, were opened wide.

"Hey, come on, it's okay now."

She seemed to recognize me then. Her screams turned into deep, tearing sobs. I helped her to her feet and helped her to dress. She was confused, bewildered; her movements were clumsy. She did not appear to notice either Murphy or Ralph. When she was fully dressed except for her boots, I got her sleeping bag, spread it on the floor near the fire, unzipped it and held it open while she crawled inside. I zipped the bag to her throat and pulled the hood up over her head.

Ralph was standing now, unsteady, wavering, holding his head where I'd hit him with the rifle stock. He staggered toward the door. I came up behind him and soccer-kicked him at the knees, scything his legs from under him, and he hit the floor hard and then slowly rolled over onto his chest. I took the laces from Murphy's boots and tightly tied Ralph's wrists and ankles.

I dumped out the contents of a rucksack and slipped it over Murphy's head and pulled the drawstring. My chest heaved spasmodically, but I did not vomit. I spread newspapers over the floor. Blood—I was so sick of seeing it, smelling it, touching it. I felt dirtied, corrupted by blood.

I grasped Murphy by his bare ankles and dragged him across the room to the door, then outside and up the icy snow ramp, slipping now, falling and getting up, dragging him out into the deep snow. I piled snow on top of his body until it was completely buried. There was really no reason to bury him.

The moon had risen above the Wolf's ridge. The sky was dotted with wispy cirrus clouds that moved from northwest to southeast; messengers of the new storm. And a great mass of cloud had gathered far below in the forest, and while I watched, it poured up through the notch like a boiling, smoky river, then gradually spread out to fill the entire valley to within a hundred yards of the cabin. It settled quietly there. Moonlight illuminated the upper levels of the cloud bank, but it was still clear where I stood, and I could look down on the clouds or up at the moon and stars. There was not much wind. The cold was like an ulcer; it ate you alive.

I returned to the cabin. The girl's eyes were closed. She breathed very slowly and deeply, sobbing on every fourth or fifth inhalation.

We would have to wait here for an hour or two. I could not ask Karen to ski down now; she had to rest.

Ralph had managed to achieve a sitting position. His hands were tied behind his back; his legs extended straight out. His head was bleeding; blood had matted his hair and smeared his right cheek. His face appeared lumpy, wrinkled, flattened. He stared at me.

I got the pistol from the table, walked out into the room, and stood above him. I aimed the pistol between his eyes. He was not afraid. I pushed the safety off with my thumb.

"What's going on?" Karen asked.

I didn't turn; I continued aiming the pistol at Ralph. "I thought you were asleep," I said to her.

"What are you doing?"

"I'm trying to kill Ralph."

"Can't you do it?"

"I don't think so," I said.

"Kill him," she said.

I could not do it. I turned, walked to the table, and sat with my back to the fire. I put the pistol aside.

"I'd like to kill him," I said. "I've tried twice. I don't know. I suppose the only thing that prevents me from killing him is that so many men who are smarter than I have said that killing is wrong. I listened, you see. I'm a sucker for anyone who appeals to my intelligence. I'm civilized—that means I've been inspired to behave a lot more decently than my nature should have permitted. I'm civilized; there are all kinds of things I'd like to do and can't."

"What is he doing?"

"Sitting on the floor, staring at me."

"Can he get us?"

"I tied him up."

"Where is Paul?"

"I took him outside, in the snow."

"Poor Paul."

"Yes."

"He wasn't what you saw today—Paul was very sensitive, very nice."

"The world can be a pretty rough place for sensitive, nice people."

"Are you sure he can't get us?"

"He's tied, and I have his pistol and the rifle."

"Watch him," she said.

"Try to rest. We'll have to ski down soon, before this storm hits."

"It's strange," she said. "I feel that I'm not me, that I'm someone else whom I don't know."

"Yes, I know what you mean. I feel the same."

"I'm partly me, but most of myself is gone, scattered I don't know where."

"You've had a bad time."

"When—when we were . . . *amusing* him—I could take that. It was nasty, but . . . because of the . . . and *then!*"

"I know."

"It's as though my life were an intricate, pretty jigsaw puzzle, and all I had to do year by year was fit each piece into the proper place. But now . . . now it seems that all of the pieces have been scattered, and a lot of them are lost, and I'll never be able to put the puzzle together correctly after this. The pattern is gone. It will never fit together the way it should."

"You'll get over this," I told her.

"Oh, I'll get by. But that isn't the point."

"What is the point, Karen?"

"Health," she said. "I was so healthy yesterday that I didn't even believe in disease. Not really."

"You'll be okay."

"I don't think you've understood me at all. I'll be okay, but I'll be different."

"Life isn't static," I said.

"Death is. I'm just trying to say that I'm not healthy anymore. I've been infected. I'm diseased now, as most people are diseased. I never believed it would happen to me."

"How old are you?"

"Nineteen."

"And you've just been expelled from the Garden."

"Yes."

"You'll eventually adjust to exile."

"Ah, now," she said. "Yes—*that's* what frightens me."

Ralph was whispering softly. I could hear the hissing of his whispers, the monotonal sibilance, but I could not understand the words. He seemed furious at first, though, then contrite, then baffled, and then furious again. He told nasty secrets to himself. I did not look at him; I did not want to face his hatred.

I had tried to soothe Karen, but I knew she was right; she was fragmented, and no matter how cleverly she reassembled herself, the cracks would always show. The terrible stress of this day and evening, the deaths, the humiliation and ferocious lunacy had shattered her ego, her integrity of self. She was in that desperate state that is often the preliminary to conversion; I would not be surprised to learn in a few months that she had gone over to evangelical Christianity or communism or Oriental mysticism, any nucleus magnetic enough to regather and hold the fragments of herself. Still, there would always be the shadow of a shadow. For the rest of her life she would at odd moments see something out of the corner of her eye. And she would turn sharply, looking for it, and see nothing. It is there and it isn't there. You look for the shadow of the shadow outside yourself, but it's inside of you, too. Maybe that's what Ralph was telling us in his whispers.

I got up and put some more logs on the fire. It was very cold. The small fireplace simply could not do its job in this kind of cold. It exhaled a little warmth into the south end of the cabin, but most of the heat went up the chimney or was simply overwhelmed by the cold that radiated from the stone walls and wood flooring. Nothing seemed to help; not the fire, the layers of winter clothing we wore. The cold seemed like a new element, a gas on the verge of liquefying or crystallizing.

I tried to enter into a state of mind where the cold did not matter. I imagined that I was floating in a warm river and the current was slowly spinning me downstream. The water was almost steaming hot and the surface was touched by eddies and ripples and whorls. Above, I created a great golden sun that sent down pulsing waves of heat. The sky was a pale, transparent blue. I invented a hawk for my sky. That sky needed a hawk, and it needed a few feathery clouds. Most of all, it needed a fiery sun, and so I made the sun bigger. It began crowding the horizons. The trees growing along the river banks were July green, and the hot wind spun and rattled the leaves of the trees. Beyond the trees some furrowed brown desert hills lay baking in the sun. Blurry heat mirages shimmered along the ridges. And beyond the brown hills were larger hills, conical and dark green with forests of fir and spruce; and farther still, some great granite spires climbed up into the clouds. The tops of the mountains were white with new snow, and glaciers, like the fingers of a hand, crawled down through the steep shadowed valleys.

For a long time I failed to create the right landscape: the river was icy, the sun refused to grow and burn—it was a glacial sun—but I kept on, and eventually I did not feel the cold. The river, the sun, the hills and mountains, my hawk—everything vanished and I slept.

SIXTEEN

I slept for about a half hour, and then the cold awakened me. The fireplace was a mass of pulsing red coals, dimming and then glowing brightly, dimming, glowing again, responding to the irregular chimney draft.

Ralph was curled up on the floor near the center of the room; his eyes were closed and his breath steamed.

I knelt on the floor and touched the girl's forehead. She opened her eyes and looked at me. The skin of her face was drawn taut over the bones; she looked forty years old.

"We've got to go down," I said.

"I'm exhausted," she said. "I'm so tired and cold."

"I know."

"I'm sick," she said. "I think I have a fever."

"We have to go."

"Can't we wait until morning?"

"No, a storm is coming in."

"I just don't think I can do it," she said.

"You have to do it, that's all."

"What about him?"

"Ralph? He'll have to come with us."

"No!"

"I'll keep his hands tied behind his back and I'll take the guns. He's a good enough skier to get down without the use of his arms, but not so good that he can get away."

"No," she said. *"Please!"*

"I'll carry the rifle and you take the pistol."

"What is he doing now?"

"He's asleep, or pretending to sleep."

"Wait," she said. "Where are you going?"

"Outside for a moment, to check the weather."

"Don't leave me alone with him, please."

"I'll check the laces before I go."

"Why don't you just kill him?"

"I tried and I couldn't do it."

"I'll do it," she said.

"Will you really?"

"Yes."

"You'll take the pistol and shoot him in the head?"

"Yes. I can do it. I want to do it."

"No, Karen. We can't do that."

"Why not?"

"Listen, I'll be outside for only a few minutes, and then we'll get ready to go down."

"I just don't think I can make it," she said.

"It's almost all downhill. We'll make it down to the jeep in an hour, ninety minutes at the most. You can keep going that much longer, can't you?"

"I suppose."

"Sure. It's your mind that wants to quit, not your body."

I checked the nylon bootlaces with which I'd tied Ralph's wrists and ankles. The lace around his wrists was so tight that his fingers were white and swollen and cold. He did not move or look at me, but his body was tense; he was awake.

I removed the bolt from his rifle and put it into my pocket; I got the pistol off the table, switched on the safety, then stuck the gun in my belt.

I went outside. The cloud bank below the cabin was gone now, but the high cirrus clouds still moved across the indigo sky in long parallel bands. The moon had risen well above the ridge. A long cloud moved beneath it now. I picked up Frank's rifle, wiped the snow from the telescope's lenses, and looked up at the dim pinpoints of stars whose light had started toward earth a billion years ago. It occurred to me that with a powerful enough telescope one might possibly stare all the way out, and back, to Creation.

I dropped the rifle into the snow beside Frank's body.

I had not noticed the light, dry touch of the cold at first, but now it began to possess me.

The moon gradually emerged from behind the tattered end of the cloud, and it was as though a rheostat were being turned up; the light slowly increased until it became as bright as a summer false dawn. The moon illuminated the clouds and reflected off the great bowl of snow. Each individual snow crystal was a bluish white spark, and the billions of surface crystals together caught the moonlight and released it, glittering with what looked like a vast electric fire. The summit of the Wolf and its snow plume sparkled in the moonlight. Shadows pooled in all the furrows and hollows. It was a stark black and white landscape, snow and shadow, the glowing moon and stars and clouds against the black sky. It looked like a photograph taken in daylight but so overexposed that all of the color had been bleached from the film. And it was static like a picture; static, hard, cold.

When I returned to the cabin the girl was standing by the table, trying to light the Primus stove. Her movements were still slow and poorly coordinated.

"Are you okay?" I asked her.

"Yes," she said dully.

"Is there any soup left?"

"No, just coffee."

"Coffee will be fine."

Ralph was sitting up now. I took the pocketknife from the table, walked over and cut the lace that tied his ankles. He closed his eyes; he would not look at me. I helped him to his feet.

"Come on over to the fire and warm up, Ralph," I said. He walked stiffly around the table and stood with his back to the fire. He closed his eyes.

"What's wrong with him?" Karen asked.

"I don't know. Maybe he's burned out, finally."

"He seems docile."

"Seems," I said. "What's wrong there?"

"I can't get the stove to light."

"Is it out of fuel?"

"No."

"Did you prime it?"

"No, I forgot."

"Pour some kerosene in the little cup and light it."

I went to the dark northeast corner of the room, got all the skis and poles and carried them back to the fireside.

"What are you going to do?" the girl asked.

"Wax up. I'll see if I can slow Ralph's skis and—"

And then I heard a remote thudding noise, like the sound of a far-off jet airplane cracking through the sound barrier.

"Oh, Christ," I said.

The girl looked at me.

"God*damn* it!" I said.

Ralph had turned and was looking at me, too; he knew that sound, and for an instant we were allies again.

The west window shattered, spraying glass into the room, and then it seemed that the cabin imploded; there was a blast of heavy wind, all the other windows blew in, and the entire hut shifted off its foundations. The floor bulged and rippled. The north wall and a large section of the east wall collapsed. Roof timbers fell; rocks flew like cannonballs; the air was filled with a choking cloud of snow and dust. The east wall seemed to disassemble piece by piece. It was like watching a strip of time-lapse photography: first the construction of the hut is filmed, each stone and plank and timber as it fits into place, and then you run the film backwards and watch the hut sequentially vanish.

The south end of the cabin, where we were, remained standing, perhaps because of the extra strength provided by the fireplace and chimney, or because of the wind blast's angle.

It was totally silent for an instant. The girl was watching me. Ralph had closed his eyes again. And then there was a hissing and crashing noise, a throbbing hum like the sound of a stormy sea. A cascading white tide of snow entered what remained of the cabin. The girl was knocked off her feet. I saw her struggling to rise against the deepening swirl of snow. Then she went under, and the two kerosene lanterns—still burning—were swept off the table and buried. The chimney wind sprayed burning coals into the room. The snow struck in successive waves, knee-high, to my thighs, my waist, twisting my body around in a complete revolution and driving me back toward the wall. I saw Ralph go under just before the remaining coals in the fireplace were covered. The room went black. Another wave of snow struck my chest, driving me off my feet and lifting me back and up against the wall. My head was free, but I held my breath for as long as I could; I feared that I might choke, drown, in the dense haze of snow particles.

The snow consolidated immediately, and I felt as though I were encased in a soft, cold plaster. The snow was packed so tightly around my body that it was difficult to expand my chest enough to fill my lungs. My head and right shoulder remained above the snow level. I heard a voice, a whimper.

"Who is it?" I said.

"Me." The girl.

"Are you okay?"

"I don't know. I think so."

"How did you get out?"

"It's just my legs—" she coughed violently for a moment—"I can't get my legs out," she said.

The last wave of snow, the one that had lifted me up against the wall, had apparently also lifted the girl, partly freeing her.

"Ralph?" I said.

The girl coughed again.

"Karen," I said.

"What?"

"Listen, don't panic."

"Oh, God," she said. "I am so tired."

"We might be able to dig our way to the surface."

"I just don't care," she said in a kind of whimper. "Really, I'm exhausted; I want to sleep. I just don't care anymore."

"Don't quit."

"What's the point?" she said.

"How deep are you buried?"

"To my hips, almost."

"And both of your hands are free? Look, dig yourself out and then come over here and help me."

She was quiet.

"Dig!" I said.

She began scraping at the snow.

The snow was firmly packed around me, but by persistent rocking back and forth and from side to side, I created enough space so that I could breathe without effort.

"Karen, how are you doing?"

"My fingers hurt. They're cold and sore."

"Keep digging."

Loose snow had infiltrated my clothing and was now melting from body heat; I was wet and cold.

After about fifteen minutes, the girl said, "All right."

"You're free?"

"Yes."

"Come here, then."

"It's so dark—where are you?"

"Just follow my voice. I'm against the wall just beyond the fireplace."

I heard rustling sounds as she crawled over the snow, and then she touched my face with her cold fingertips.

"Is it you?" she asked, and there was a hint of panic in her voice.

"Yes."

"Where is *he?*"

"I saw Ralph go under."

"Are you sure?"

"Yes, he went under and was driven back toward the fireplace."

She was breathing rapidly.

"We're going to get out of here," I said. "You'll see."

"Will we really?"

"Yes, I promise you. Just don't panic."

"There isn't enough air."

"Yes there is."

"I'm suffocating."

"No, there is plenty of air."

"I can't breathe."

"The snow is porous. We don't have to worry about air."

"I can't *breathe!*"

"Relax," I said. "Listen to me! Relax. You have plenty of air. Do you hear? You're *not* suffocating!"

She was breathing swiftly and deeply. "I can't breathe," she said. "I'm dizzy."

"You're hyperventilating. Listen, it's all in your mind. You mustn't panic this way. I promise you that I won't lie to you about anything. I'll tell you exactly how we stand at all times. All right? Do you hear me? I'm not lying to you—we have all the air we need. Do you believe me?"

"Yes. Yes. Yes. Oh God!"

"Now, start digging around my arms first, and when my hands are free I can begin helping you."

"I can't breathe. I can't breathe. I can't breathe."

"Dig, Karen!"

"My fingers are numb. My fingers are frozen. I can't breathe. I can't breathe."

"Dig!"

She began clawing at the snow. Her breath hissed.

"Fine," I said. "Don't hurry; we have time. Slow down, take it easy. You have plenty of air."

It seemed to take a long time to free my arms, but then, with me helping, we were able to dig a funnel-shaped hole around my chest. Once that was done, the rest was comparatively easy; I could exert leverage then, pull myself upward, squirm and claw and kick, and soon I managed to crawl out of the snow, and I was free. My hands ached with the cold.

"Are you okay?" I asked.

"My hands . . . I can't feel them anymore."

"Put them inside your jacket," I said. "Beneath your armpits."

"It's so dark," she said.

"I had Ralph's flashlight. Maybe . . ." The zipper pocket on my jacket had been closed, and I hadn't lost the flashlight. I gripped it carefully with my numbed fingers and flicked on the beam. The small snow cavern seemed to explode with light; it blazed with millions of pinpoint reflections, and my eyes, adjusted to the darkness, were temporarily blinded.

We were trapped in a domed ice pocket roughly the size of an igloo. Two roof beams and some splintered oak planks showed through the snow five feet above our heads. I could see the stones of the upper section of chimney.

"What can we do?" the girl cried.

"Be quiet. Let me think."

"You promised to tell me the truth."

"I know. Please, let me think for a moment."

The snow overhead could be twenty feet deep or sixty feet deep. We could try to tunnel our way out and hope that the surface was not too far away, was within the limits of our strength. We could wait for a rescue party. Snow was good insulation, and our body heat would warm this small space; we could survive here for several days if we had to.

"Okay," I said. "First we'll get this area organized. Then we'll start digging a tunnel."

"It won't work," she said.

"If we're too deep to tunnel out of here, we can just sit tight and wait for a rescue crew. We're overdue in town now—they'll know for sure something is wrong when we don't turn up tomorrow morning. They'll get a crew up here to dig us out."

"You promised you wouldn't lie to me."

"I'm not lying. I don't say they'll be here tomorrow, but they *might*. The storm could slow them down. It may even be that we'll have to remain here for a couple days, but we can last."

"I have claustrophobia," she said.

"Everyone does. Do you think I like this?"

"You won't lie," she said, fighting against hysteria. "You promised me you wouldn't lie."

"We have a good chance, a very good chance."

"How good?"

"About eighty-twenty in our favor," I lied.

"You swear it?"

"I swear. Are your hands warm now?"

"They're still cold, and they hurt."

"We'll wait a little while longer and then start digging. Beneath the snow are a lot of things we need—the sleeping bags, our mittens, food, the stove, the lanterns, clothing. We're going to dig them out."

"My hands are so sore."

"The planks sticking through the snow up there will make fair shovels."

"But won't the roof collapse if you take them?"

"No, they aren't holding up the snow. The snow has consolidated; it won't fall on us."

"Are you sure?"

"I'll give you the flashlight. You shine it on the ceiling while I pry out a couple of the boards. Don't be frightened if a little snow sifts down. Then you start digging right about there, where the edge of the table was. Okay?"

"Okay."

"Good girl. You'll see, everything will—wait. Did you hear that?"

"What?"

I heard it again, a low groaning sound, coming from somewhere below me and to my right.

"It's Ralph," I said.

"Ralph!"

"He's alive."

"No, it's impossible."

I heard the noise again. Karen heard it, too.

"I'll dig him out," I said.

"But why should you want to save *him?*"

"I really don't know."

"It's stupid. Let him die, for God's sake, let him die!"

"Look, it's partly personal. I was buried in the snow once and Ralph helped to dig me out."

"And you think you owe him a favor?" the girl asked incredulously.

"Anyway, when they taught me that human life was sacred, they forgot the qualifications."

"And *his* life is sacred?" she asked, staring at me.

"No," I said. "Here, take the flashlight."

SEVENTEEN

I used a four-foot-long, eight-inch-wide oak plank as a shovel. The splintered, beveled edge penetrated the snow fairly easily, and I was able to scoop out a couple pounds of snow with each try. I dug down directly in front of the fireplace. I worked steadily and rhythmically and soon I was sweating and a hot ache had begun to burn in my injured shoulder.

By the time I had dug a pit three-and-one-half feet deep, the girl had excavated one of the sleeping bags, a stove, three mittens, a rucksack (mine), and one of the kerosene lanterns. The glass shield was broken, but the lantern worked; a match was touched to the wick, there was a sputtering as the wetness burned away, and then the flame swelled and curved into a glowing harp-shaped blaze, and the snow dome filled with light.

"Have you found him?" Karen asked.

"No."

"Can you hear him?"

"No."

"Good."

"I think he was driven back into the fireplace."

"I'm tired," she said. "My hands are freezing."

"Warm a pair of mittens over the lantern."

"What shall we do with all the loose snow we've dug up?"

"Pack it around the walls."

And so our tiny dome of space decreased in circumference as it increased in depth.

I kept digging. Soon the hole was wide enough so that I could lower my body down into it and still continue shoveling.

I rested again. "Christ," I said, "I should have found him by now. He was just about here when he went under."

"What does it matter?"

"He has to be inside the fireplace."

"He's dead."

"Maybe not."

"He has to be dead; he's been down there a long time, more than an hour."

"No, he could still be alive."

"You haven't heard him for a long time, have you?"

"No."

"He's dead."

"You have no idea what it's like to be buried alive."

"Dig, then," she said. "I don't care."

I found him. The force of the final wave of snow had driven him, on his back, headfirst into the fireplace and then partway up the chimney. His head had stayed above the level of snow, and so he had been able to breathe.

Some of the burning coals had been blown out into the room, but others had been lifted by the snow, and they had pressed against his right thigh. The snow had not immediately extinguished the coals; his thigh was deeply burned, and after we had raised him out of the hole I'd dug in the snow (the girl pulling, I lifting, pushing), my hands were covered with a warm greasy substance with the texture of melted cheese. His flesh had peeled off, stuck to my hands.

He lay supine on the snow platform. He was conscious; his eyes were open and he lifted his head and looked at us, but he made no sound. His thigh, framed by an oval of burnt-edged fabric, was raw and blistered and glistening moistly in the lantern light. I could smell his burned flesh. I covered the burns with loose snow.

Karen Bright coldly returned his gaze. "Now," she said, "when we find food, we'll have to share it with him."

I scrubbed my hands with snow. I could not remove the grease from my fingers.

"Let's blind him," she said.

I looked at her.

"His eyes," she said.

"What? What did you say?"

"I'll do it."

"What are you talking about?"

"You don't have to help me."

Except for the steady, metallic intensity of her stare, there was no expression on her face, no distortion; and her voice was smooth, wheedling.

"You'll *blind* him?"

"I found the knife," she said. "I'll do it."

"Karen, no! For Christ's sake, you'll be talking about cannibalism tomorrow. Listen, we have to keep our heads. We must survive, but let's try to stay halfway human while we're doing it."

"You're wrong," she said coolly. "Those old rules don't apply anymore."

"Give me the knife."

"No."

"Give it to me."

She handed me the knife. I pushed Ralph over on his side and cut the laces which bound his hands. His fingers were white, swollen, hard. He cupped them, lifted them to his mouth and began breathing on them.

"You cut him loose!" the girl cried.

"Let's keep digging," I said. "We need the supplies."

"He'll kill us!"

"His hands will be useless for an hour."

Ralph lifted his head and watched the girl. And then he slowly reached out and touched her hand. She gasped, recoiled. There had been nothing gentle in his gesture, nor anything hostile; it seemed to be a simple expression of curiosity, an inquiry, perhaps, into warmth and texture.

"What does he want?"

"I don't know. I think's he's gone all the way over the edge."

"I don't want him to touch me."

"He doesn't even seem to know that he's in terrific pain. He's probably on the way to the droolers' ward."

Ralph turned his head and gazed at me. Despite all he had been through—his fatigue, the physical battering he'd taken, being buried beneath the snow for ninety minutes, his burns—there were no lines visible on his face, no apparent muscular tension, no attempt to control his expression; he looked like a simple-minded child. It was as though a final murder, a suicide, had obliterated the dominant side of his personality, and what remained was new, hardly used, unformed. He had attained a spurious innocence.

I had left the oak plank in the fireplace. I slid down, ducked my head and looked around. Light, an almost imperceptible shine that seemed independent of the lantern. A few snowflakes drifted down the chimney. I looked up: a dull luminescence, a faint draft, several stars. The avalanche mound was not nearly so thick as I'd supposed; the top of the chimney was clear.

The chimney narrowed as it rose; the square of light at the top appeared large enough to permit the girl to get through, though it looked as if it might be an impossibly tight squeeze for me.

I backed out of the fireplace, stood up. Ralph lay quietly on the snow, his eyes closed. The girl was still drawn up against the curved white wall.

"The top of the chimney protrudes beyond the avalanche cone," I said. "We can get out. You can, anyway."

"You promised you wouldn't lie to me," she said.

"Stop playing that record. Let yourself hope. It's going to be an awfully tight squeeze. We'll have to take off all our clothes except the long underwear, and maybe even that. No, we'll wear our boots; we'll need them to climb the chimney."

"It must be too small," she said.

"It's small, all right, especially at the top, but I know you can do it, and I intend to try. When you get out, I'll pass up your clothing and ski equipment, and mine, too, if it looks as if I'll be able to make it."

"What about him?"

"He can't go anywhere with that leg. We'll leave him here in the sleeping bag. A rescue party can dig him out."

"What if I can crawl through the chimney and you can't?"

"Then you decide. Either ski down to the valley by yourself—I'll give you the keys to Frank's jeep—or you can return here and help me dig a tunnel to the surface. It isn't that far."

She nodded slowly.

"Okay. Now you start digging over there, toward the corner where I stacked the ski equipment. I'll have to go back down and remove the damper plate. As soon as I've finished I'll come back up and help you."

"Can I really get out?"

"Yes."

She smiled.

Ralph had tucked his hands inside his down jacket. The snow I had piled on his burned thigh was melting and turning a pinkish color. He lifted his head and looked at us as if he had not the slightest notion of who we were and he could not understand what he was doing in this strange, cold, white place with two strangers.

I cleared the chimney and then helped Karen finish digging out the ski equipment. Ralph's rifle was in the corner, too. We could not find the pistol; it had been stuck in my belt when the avalanche struck and then lost in the waves of snow.

"Are you ready, Karen?"

"Yes."

"Start getting undressed."

"Not while *he's* watching."

"Look, I know what you went through tonight. But you'll be wearing your long underwear, and anyway he can't hurt you with his eyes."

"He has already hurt me with his eyes."

"Is that why you wanted to blind him? Jesus, you're turning into a character out of a Greek myth. Okay, undress down in the snow pit here and pass me your clothes. He won't be able to see you. Keep your boots on, as I said. The chimney is made of blocks of stone, and so you shouldn't have too much trouble finding hand- and footholds. When you get outside, I'll climb the chimney to where it narrows and pass you your clothing, and then I'll try it."

"All right."

"Good girl. You'll be drinking a hot buttered rum in about two hours."

Her hips jammed at the top of the chimney, but she squirmed and kicked and finally dragged herself free. Then I could see her face framed in the dull square of light as she looked down at me.

"You'll never make it," she said. Her voice was deepened and amplified by the chimney.

"Are any of the chimney rocks loose?"

"I don't think so."

"Try to pry a couple out of the mortar. If you can remove two or three of the rocks, the rest should come away easily."

"I'm cold," she said.

"Wait." I made a compact bundle of her clothes, climbed the chimney until it was uncomfortably close around my shoulders, and then, balancing, extended the bundle upward.

"I can't reach it," she said.

"Try—lean down."

The bundle was lifted from my hand. I retreated back down to the fireplace. I could see a few stars, a moonlit cloud, and then the girl's face reappeared in the square of light.

"Try to work some stones loose," I said. "I'll go back inside, in case you knock some rocks down here."

"It won't work," she said.

"It might. Listen, the avalanche pretty thoroughly destroyed the hut; it might have loosened the chimney stones, too. Even if it didn't, you might be able to kick them loose. Try, try hard! Get leverage, lie on your back in the snow and push, kick with your feet. Chip the mortar loose with the spike of your ski pole. Give it everything you have, Karen. Don't just say it won't work—*try it!*"

"Okay."

I backed out of the fireplace and climbed up onto the small platform of snow. Ralph had not changed position. His face was smooth, tranquil in the lantern light.

I gently brushed away the loose snow covering his burns. The wounds were raw, deeply pitted, blistered, crusted around the edges, still oozing a clear, pinkish fluid.

A rock fell down into the fireplace, then another. The girl shouted triumphantly. More rocks fell.

I removed my jacket, the wool shirt, and the light cashmere sweater, and then I took my pocketknife and cut the sweater into long strips. Ralph watched me curiously as I bound the burns on his leg. He did not wince or cry out. I did not see how his pain could have been cut off by some neural dysfunction, so it had to be psychological, perhaps some kind of hysterical or autohypnotic reaction.

More rocks fell into the fireplace. The girl shouted.

As soon as I finished wrapping Ralph's leg, I realized that I had made a mistake; it would have been better to leave the wounds exposed, or covered lightly with snow. Well, I had done nearly everything wrong during the last thirty-one or thirty-two hours; another mistake was merely consistent.

I got the two sets of skis and poles, passed them up to the girl and then returned to the little snow room.

"I'm taking the flashlight," I said to Ralph. "You'll have the lantern, but it will probably exhaust its fuel in an hour or so. You'll be alone in the dark then, but it won't be so bad, Ralph. You'll be okay until help arrives."

He suddenly smiled at me; a stiff, utterly insincere smile, a mockery of a smile.

I wondered what it meant, and then I felt that same stiff smile on my own face; he was mimicking me without parody. He was trying out a phony, sympathetic smile.

I slipped down into the excavation.

He lifted his head. "Jack."

"You know my name?"

"Of course. Jesus Christ, I've known you for years."

"Well," I said, "you've seemed pretty remote for the last hour or so."

"I've been on an astral voyage," he said.

I looked at him.

"My soul was projected to strange, beautiful times and planets, Jack. I married nine times and had one hundred sons. The crystals are clouded, Jack; I was caught in a terrible meteor storm. My leg has been burned by a hail of small meteors. While I was gone the men in cardigan sweaters drilled a small hole in my head."

"That will teach you to not astrally project, Ralph. Stay home and tend the store in the future."

"I don't want to stay here," he said.

"Neither do I, Ralph."

"Jack, you've done terrible things to me."

"Yes?"

"I'll forgive you if you don't leave me here. I can't stand it here, Jack; bad things are happening. I've had dreams."

"Hang on," I said. "I'm going."

"Jack!"

"What?"

He had returned from a pleasant interlude of astral projection, and now, once again, his face was gray and cold and rigid with hatred.

"Jack," he said, and his voice sounded like a file rasping against metal, "I'll get you for this even if it costs me Paradise."

EIGHTEEN

The girl had removed the stones and mortar from the top two feet of the chimney. I passed my rucksack up to her and then crawled out onto the avalanche mound.

The moon was almost directly overhead now, and it spread a pale, even light over the otherworldly landscape. The big cirque was still divided into stark blacks and whites, but the shadows had shortened, become compactly angular, and the high mountain ridges and peaks surrounding us were sharply defined against the blue-black sky. Stars vanished behind clouds, reappeared. A vaporous ring encircled the moon.

It was snowing lightly. I looked up; the sky was clear except for the high, stringy cirrus clouds. It was snowing where we stood, all around us, though it might not be snowing a few hundred feet above: the night was so cold that the moisture in the air was crystallizing and falling as frost.

The avalanche mound was hard, compacted into snow-ice, and there were cabin timbers, planks, wall stones, boulders and rocks, and tufts of dried yellow alpine grass scattered everywhere. The Wolf had been swept clean; not just the new storm, but right down to the earth. The avalanche had started just below the summit and had gradually fanned out until it reached a half mile in width. Most of its force had already been spent when the forward edge struck the cabin. I could see the track of another small avalanche to the north. We were not out of danger: the snow was very unstable; it could avalanche anywhere along the Wolf's long ridge.

The girl stood nearby, shivering and breathing huge clouds of vapor. She was in her skis.

"What is he doing down there?" she asked.

"Ralph? God knows—maybe preparing for a different dimension of awareness."

Karen had found three mittens in the cabin; I had one of them. I went through my rucksack and got out an extra pair of wool stockings. I could use one for a mitten.

"Do you have a scarf or muffler or anything?"

"No," she said.

"Take this stocking and tie it around the lower part of your face. Skiing is going to create a wind, and you could get frostbite. You don't want to lose your nose, do you?"

She took the stocking. "What will you do?"

"I've got eyeholes in my cap. I'll just pull it down over my face."

"My God, it's cold!" she said.

It was cold, and so quiet we could hear the falling snow crackle as it hit the ground.

I cleared my boots of loose snow, stepped into the binding of my right ski and locked the cable.

"Stay away from the avalanche snow," I said. "It'll be hard and lumpy, difficult skiing. Stay in the powder."

She nodded.

I stepped into my left ski, turned the clamp. "How well do you ski?"

She handed me my ski poles. "Pretty well."

"How well?"

"I've done some racing."

"Powder snow?"

"I've skied powder, yes."

"Okay. Now the incline is gradual for the first couple of miles. You could probably take it straight, but we can't take a chance of an injury or equipment breakage. Just think about how it would be to walk eight or nine miles through deep snow in this cold. If you break a leg . . ."

"I understand," she said.

"Okay then, stay in control at all times."

"How far is it to the jeep?"

"About eleven miles."

"So far?" she asked.

"On an ordinary day at a ski area you'd ski eleven miles before lunch. Except for that one long, steep hill ahead—you can see it from here—the run is all downhill. Now go ahead. Ski carefully. I'll follow you."

She pushed off with her poles, took a few ice-skating steps and dipped down the hard snow of the avalanche mound, gaining speed. She was moving swiftly when she hit the deep snow. She was not prepared for the abrupt deceleration and almost fell; the snow erupted in a powdery haze which sparkled in the moonlight, and for an instant I lost sight of her, but then I picked her up twenty yards down the slope. It looked as though she had been cut off at the waist—a torso gliding silently through an element like smoke. The snow around her body undulated, curled back; snow particles were left hanging in the air behind her like a shot-silk haze. Her track was shadowed, a dark line carved through the moonlit snow. She turned then, a good wide-arced sweeping turn, passed back around through the fall line and then turned once again; her track then became a straight line with an almost perfect S at the end. She was a good skier. We would be all right.

I pulled down my stocking cap and then started downhill, away from what remained of the hut. For an instant I thought of Ralph, and then I left him behind. My skis rasped on the hard snow of the avalanche mound, chattered as I went through an area of icy lumps; and then I hit the powder snow. I felt the impact against my thighs, slowing me, throwing my upper body forward. The snow softly exploded around me, as if a mine had blown up at my feet, enclosing me in the blizzard, and then I skied through it, and below me I could see the whiteness stretching away endlessly and, far down the slope, the girl, now just an angular shadow at the end of a snaking, ever-extending dark line through the snow. My eyes watered from the cold. There was a silky hissing noise, no louder than a whisper. I was gaining speed now, and my skis rode higher in the snow. I blinked away the tears. Ahead, I saw the beginning of the girl's S track, and I turned the other way, lifting, unweighting, leaning away from the centrifugal force, and I closed the S at the center, turned again and made the S into an 8. I quickly glanced over my shoulder; it was a good 8, nearly symmetrical. The snow hanging in the air behind me was dully rainbowed in the moonlight.

A cloud passed under the moon and I skied through darkness for a few moments, and then the light gradually returned. My legs were beginning to tire. I was gaining on the girl; she was about fifty yards ahead of me now. She turned to look back at me over her shoulder, and then all at once she went down; she simply vanished, and a thirty-foot plume spurted out of the snow.

There was a deep hole where she'd hit, and then a long trench. I stopped just below her. She was two-thirds buried in the snow and struggling to free herself.

"Are you all right?" I asked.

She brushed the snow off her face and neck. "I caught a tip," she said.

"You aren't hurt?"

"I don't think so. No. Wow! I was going so fast, and then I lost it and I was flying through the air, and then I was *submerged.*" She fell back into the snow. "It's comfortable here."

"We'd better check your skis," I said.

"In a moment."

"That snow is cold."

"Warmer than the air," she said.

"You'll get your clothes wet and they'll lose insulation. We still have miles to go."

"'And miles to go before I sleep,'" she said.

"Come on." I helped her to her feet. There had been no damage to her skis or bindings. She leaned against me while she brushed the snow from her boots and bindings, and then awkwardly stepped into the bindings and clamped them.

"How much farther?" she asked.

"Still a long ways. We have to climb the hill up ahead. That will take us about fifteen minutes, but then it's a long run down to the forest."

"My legs feel like jelly."

"Are you cold?"

"I didn't notice the cold while I was skiing, but I'm starting to get cold again."

"We'd better get moving."

"That was lovely skiing," she said.

"Beautiful."

"It made me feel healthy again. Do you remember when I told you that I was diseased and that I would never be healthy again? Well, that's not *completely* true."

"Of course not."

"There may be times when it affects me, but not too often."

"That's right, Karen."

"Right now, though, I feel so good that it makes me ashamed, a little guilty. You know?"

"It's okay to be happy," I said, smiling at her.

"I mean, it seems, I don't know—*stonehearted* not to mourn. For myself, too, in a way—not just the others."

"Stop thinking," I said. "Just ski."

"Fine, yes."

"Get up speed now and ski as high on the hill as you can. We'll have to herringbone or sidestep to the top."

"Righto," she said, and she started off.

It took twice as long as I had estimated to climb the hill, a half hour instead of fifteen minutes, because she was tired and had to stop often to rest.

We reached the top of the hill. I looked back over the Columbine Meadows, following our tracks with my eyes until they vanished into the shadows. The great bowl of mountains shone phosphorescently in the moonlight. In the other direction, to the south, I could look down over the narrowing valley beyond the notch to the dark forest below. And farther off I could see another chain of mountains, the peaks rising like islands out of a sea of clouds.

"What a marvelous night," she said. "If only it weren't so cold."

"Yes."

"Where is this storm you've been talking about?"

"It's coming."

"My toes are numb," she said.

"We'd better go," I said.

"No, I want to rest. Please?"

"Okay."

"Look," she said. "There's the Big Dipper, and Polaris."

"Yes."

"Is that Venus? Over there—do you see?"

"Yes, it is."

"The Roman goddess of love and beauty," she said. "Venus. I wonder if what happened back there ruined me."

"Ruined you?"

"For sex, I mean."

"Oh. Well, we can always go to a motel and find out."

She laughed.

"I'm partly serious," I said.

"How serious?"

"Fifty-one percent serious."

She laughed again. "Too bad. I'm only forty-nine percent willing."

"I'm lucky at cards, though," I said.

"Listen, do you suppose—oh, no," she said. "Oh, God, please, no."

"What is it?"

"It's him! Back there."

"What? Who? Listen, Karen—"

"It's him! Look, my God, he's coming after us!"

"What the hell!" I turned and looked back toward the cabin. "Ralph?"

"Yes! Yes!"

"It can't be."

"There!" she cried.

I would not have seen him if he had not been moving; he was far away, above our figure-eight track in the snow, but a new track was being unraveled, and at the tip there was a shadow, a man. I could not believe that he was able to ski on his burned leg.

"He's coming!" she cried, and she started toward the edge.

I grabbed her arm. "Listen," I said. "Wait, listen to me."

She struggled wildly.

"Karen, listen."

"Please, oh please let me go!"

"Don't panic. We have a moment. Are you listening to me?"

She started to cry.

I shook her roughly. "Take the keys to the jeep," I said.

"What? What? Look, he's coming after us!"

"Here, take them."

She accepted the keys.

"Wait now! Here's the flashlight. You'll need it in the forest."

She hurriedly put the keys and flashlight into her jacket pocket.

"Wait, now—listen to me. Frank's and my tracks are still in the snow from yesterday. Do you see them? *Karen, do you see them?*"

"Yes, yes, please hurry, please."

"Follow the tracks all the way down. They'll lead you to the jeep. Do you hear? Drive into town. If the jeep doesn't start, keep going down the road; it will take you to the main highway."

"Yes, yes."

"You must keep your head."

"Look!"

I turned and saw Ralph skidding to a stop. He vanished in the cloud of snow, and then the snow settled and I saw him again. He was only a few hundred yards away now.

"He's got the rifle!" Karen cried.

"It's useless," I said. "I have the bolt."

I heard a soft fluttering in the air and then the sharp crack of the rifle.

"Go!" I shouted.

She slid forward and then dipped down off the top of the hill. She immediately dropped into a racing tuck.

NINETEEN

I scrambled forward, digging with the poles, and dipped down over the rim. The top part of the hill was steep, and in just a few seconds I had overcome the inertial drag and was going very fast. My eyes blurred. My ski tips rose up out of the snow. The snow hissed, sizzled with a sound like fat frying in a pan. Karen was about sixty feet ahead of me. The moonlight did not reach this side of the hill, and she was just a dark swift shadow against the paler shadow on the snow. She rose out of her tuck just above the base of the hill, straightening to absorb the shock from the sudden change of gradient with her knees, and then she flashed out of the shadow and into moonlight again. She checked her speed once, twice, and long rooster tails of snow spurted up from her skis.

A half mile ahead I could see the moon-bright, steeply rising slopes of the entrance notch. We would have to run down the center between the two slopes, and there was a serious danger that our skis cutting through the snow would break the surface tension and bring an avalanche down on us.

We lost speed on the runout but were still going very fast, flying at the edge of control. There was a thick lump of ice on the part of the wool stocking cap which covered my mouth, where my exhalations had frozen. The tears froze on my eyelashes, restricting my vision; all I saw was the sparkling blur of whiteness.

The valley narrowed. Karen Bright lost her balance for an instant and then recovered. And then, peripherally, I saw the whiteness rising quickly on either side; we were moving into the upper section of the notch.

We went straight down the chute. Ahead, below the entrance to the V-slot, where the ridges merged with the gently rounded hills of the lower valley, I could see the dark mass of forest. The grade leveled out for fifty yards and then steepened again. I saw one of the dwarfed, wind-stripped trees, then another. We were almost through the notch. Karen began checking her speed. She was following our tracks from yesterday morning, and if she stayed with them she could not become lost; they would lead her down the steep switchbacks of the forest trail all the way to the jeep.

I turned to the right and curved around, temporarily blinded by the snow spray, to the beginning of the ridge. Momentum carried me forty or fifty feet up the slope. I had to rest for a moment, the muscles of my right thigh were trembling violently. I looked down and saw the girl weaving in and out of the scrub trees, checking her speed with every turn, and then, moving slowly now, she glided off into the darkness of the forest.

I started climbing the ridge, heading north, back toward the Wolf. The snow was deep and loose, and it seemed that I slid back a yard for every two or three yards I gained. Ralph was probably climbing the hill above the notch now, where Karen and I had been standing when he shot at us. He would be slowed by his injured leg. Ralph and I were engaged in a hill-climbing race now, though I tried not to think of that; I wanted to climb as smoothly and rhythmically as possible—panic, hurrying too much, would only exhaust me.

I was not certain that I was doing the right thing. Perhaps I should have gone with the girl. We might have reached the jeep before Ralph. That wasn't certain, though; Ralph was a superb skier, much better than Karen and I, and he would have skied the trail through the trees far more quickly than we could. He would have gained on us through the forest. And even so, I doubted that the jeep would start after being out in this terrible cold for so long. Ralph could follow our tracks, gaining all the time, and he had the rifle.

My legs were deadened, numbed from the effort, and I could feel a pain growing in my side. My breath whistled on the exhalations.

The rifle. I could not understand that. I had left his rifle behind in the hut, but its bolt was in my pocket. Frank's rifle was buried beneath tons of snow. I knew that Ralph had taken the bolt to Frank's gun; perhaps the two rifles were of the same make and model—no, that wasn't true; I remembered now that they had been different. Then maybe the two rifles were close enough in design so that the bolts were interchangeable. That had to be it. But Christ, what rotten luck!

I simply had to rest. Just for a moment, I promised myself, to the count of thirty. I leaned over my ski poles and breathed deeply. There was a phlegmy sound in my lungs. My mouth was dry, with a metallic taste. The muscles of my right thigh were still jumping. My shoulders were sore and my lower back ached.

I cocked my head and looked down over my tracks. I had gained about two hundred vertical feet of altitude. The forest was spread out below me, rolling downward in a series of ever-diminishing hills. I could see the white line of the creek snaking down through the shadows. The upper branches of the trees shone a greenish-gold color in the moonlight, like the glow of organic decay.

I resumed climbing. The grade steepened and I had to begin sidestepping. I could hear the thumping of my heart. Blood throbbed in my ears. The air had a burnt taste. My limbs were dead.

I reached the top of the steep section. The ridge dipped here, ran almost level for eighty yards and then resumed its long, irregular climb to the summit of the Wolf.

I rested again; I had to. Behind and below me, the ridge, the hilly dark forest, miles of treeless white fields, the highway (I could see a car's headlights moving slowly through the far-off darkness), and then more fields, more forest, rising to the distant mountain range. The lower slopes of those mountains were still shrouded in clouds; the peaks blazed whitely in the moonlight.

Down and to my right, the floor of the V-notch—I could see the shadowed tracks cutting through the snow.

Ahead, above eye level and slightly to my right, I could see the hill.

I skied down the slight incline and then hurried along the level stretch. There was time. I had covered two-thirds of the level section when I saw a figure rise to the top of the other hill and stand silhouetted in the moonlight. I dropped flat in the snow. He would rest for a moment; so would I.

I threw my ski poles aside. I did not want them if I was caught in the avalanche. There was a deep, burning sensation in my right thigh. I removed the mitten from my hand and began to knead the muscles. A cloud passed beneath the moon. I pulled off my stocking cap and picked the tiny ice balls out of my eyelashes. The cloud passed and Ralph was still a thin straight shadow against the night sky. I could taste a wet saltiness. I explored with my tongue and found that I had bitten clear through my lip. The muscles of my thigh began to flutter again. I beat them with my fist. My eyes seemed to be covered with a transparent black film; my vision dimmed. Jesus, I was falling to pieces.

The silhouette, Ralph, seemed to levitate for a moment, and then he was dropping down the smooth, shadowed face of the hill.

I slowly rose to my feet. He would not see me; his eyes were watering, and he was concentrating on the terrain ahead.

I put on my mitten, and kick-turned so that I faced in the opposite direction, toward the forest. I glanced over my shoulder: Ralph was nearing the base of the hill now, running it straight, and then he blasted out of shadow and into moonlight. A long plume of snow hovered in the air behind him. I tried to calculate his speed. I chose my angle. The moon dimmed briefly, grew bright again.

I had deliberately skied off avalanches in the past. It was safe enough if you picked your spot: you cut the slope at a sharp angle, at high speed, and ahead you had the shelter of trees or a huge pile of boulders. You could not fall, of course. You had to be correct in your selection of angle. No one outruns a dry snow avalanche—it's impossible; but you can sometimes ski beyond the edge. You cut the slope and started the avalanche, but by the time it had gained momentum you were safely out of the way.

This was different. There were no trees ahead, no rocks, no shelter until I had passed beyond the low end of the ridge. Two hundred yards, at least. This was not wholly a matter of judgment and skill. I knew that the snow was unstable, ready to avalanche, but I could not predict exactly when and how it would begin moving. I had to pick the right angle, and I had to stay on my skis, but the rest was luck.

Ralph was entering the notch. His rifle was slung over his shoulder. He used his ski poles lightly, delicately, for rhythm, and controlled his speed with short heel thrusts.

When he was about a hundred yards north of me, I pushed off the ridge. Too slow, much too slow. I steepened the angle and turned my skis down the fall line, and then, when I was going faster, I readjusted. I glanced over my shoulder. He was rapidly gaining on me; I had miscalculated his speed. I shouted, hoping to distract him—maybe he would fall. Below, out of the corner of my eye, I saw him start to pass, but then gravity took hold of me and I was skiing down the slope at a forty-five-degree angle, flying now, the bottoms of my skis just skimming the snow, and Ralph fell behind.

And then the snow ahead of me swelled up, rose into a smooth oval mound that was suddenly shattered by a spider web of dark cracks. The entire slope billowed, rolled like a stormy sea, and dark cracks zigzagged through the snow like bolts of lightning. I heard a thumping noise behind me, and then a sound like heavy rain on a pavement. The snow burst into a pit thirty feet before me and then almost immediately closed, and I passed over it and into another area of heaving snow. A boiling mass sucked me down to my waist, my hips, but then it released me. My bindings had not released, and I was still, somehow, riding the plastically swelling and shrinking waves of snow. The air was filled with glittering crystals. There was a sound like the rapids of a river, a crashing and humming, and the whole world swept downward, surging crazily, sank back, and then exploded again.

And then I was out of it. The air was fogged with a blinding, choking white haze, but the snow beneath my skis was smooth now, no longer moving beneath me.

I passed into the clear night air, and then my body quit. I fell. I skidded through the deep snow, stopped finally, and lay there, half-buried, looking back toward the notch. The moon illuminated the great cloud of snow, dimly in the center and brightly around the edges. The cloud filled the notch and spread, billowing like smoke, crawling up and out to darken the stars. I could not believe that I was alive. I should not have survived that avalanche.

A light breeze carried snow down toward me: the flakes misted the air and crackled lightly as they fell. I slowly got up and brushed off my clothes. Through the haze I could see the tall, dark conical shapes of some big trees.

"Jack."

I turned to my left, toward the voice. He was only about twenty feet away from me. Snow fell all around us. There was just enough light to bring out the orange color of his jacket. His face was a pale blur. The front lens of the telescopic sight glinted, a small yellow moon reflecting the greater moon.

"Bye-bye, Jacky," he said.

I leaped sideways, and simultaneously I heard the deep cracking thunder of the rifle and saw two flashes of yellowish-red light, a thin spurt from the muzzle and a larger, brighter flame behind it.

Ralph fell back. He started to scream, shrilly, like a cat, but the scream was abruptly cut off, and he was silent.

The bolt, designed for another rifle, had worked once, but on this second shot it had jumped loose and been driven back into his right eye. His left eye was open and gleamed moistly. Two inches of the cylindrical bolt protruded from his right eye. The blood slowly spread down over one half of his face like a black, viscid shadow.

"You aren't dead, Ralph," I said. "You have only been released to a higher plane of awareness."

* * *

The jeep had not started. Karen Bright was curled up on the back seat. She screamed when she saw me peering in through the frosted window, thinking that I was Ralph, and then she came outside and embraced me, laughing and weeping.

It was late and snowing heavily by the time we reached the highway. We finally got a ride with a salesman of pharmaceutical supplies. He told us that we were foolish to hitchhike, especially at this time of night. "Don't you know there are a lot of maniacs running around loose these days?"

AVAILABLE MAY 2013

JACKSTRAW

MUNDIAL

I assembled the rifle and secured the telescope to its mounting. The bolt worked with a smooth metallic *snick*. The rifle smelled of steel and oil and wood polish and, faintly, burnt gunpowder. It was the smell of my past, the smell of my future.

At dawn I moved to an open window. A woman, wrapped and hooded by a ropy shawl, walked diagonally across the paving stones toward the cathedral. She flushed a flock of pigeons which swirled like confetti before settling. A limping yellow dog came out of the shadows and began chasing the birds. He had no chance. He knew it; the pigeons knew it. Finally the dog shamefully limped away down an alley.

I went into the bathroom and washed my face with tap water the color of weak tea. The cracked mirror fractured my image into half a dozen oblique planes, like a Cubist portrait, and gave my eyes a crazed slant.

Sunlight had illuminated the parapet and pediment of the National Palace. People were filtering into the great plaza now: churchgoers, early celebrants, lottery ticket salesmen and shoeshine boys, beggars, men pushing wheeled charcoal braziers and food carts. An old man filled colored balloons from a helium tank. Boys kicked around a soccer ball. Policemen in pairs cruised like sharks among schools of bait fish.

Now and then I heard the voices of people passing by in the corridor. A door slammed, a woman laughed, elevator doors hissed open. This was for many an ordinary workday; they would observe the ceremony from their office windows, witnesses to pseudo history.

Blue smoke uncoiling from charcoal fires hung in the air like spiral nebulae. The cathedral's copper-sheathed dome, green with verdigris, glowed like fox-fire in the hazy sunlight. At ten o'clock the church bells again tolled, a loud off-pitch clanging whose vibrations continued—like ghosts of sound—to hum in the air ten seconds after the clangor had ceased. Two cops dragged a rowdy young man into the shade beneath the east side colonnade and began beating him with their clubs.

Members of a band were gathering on the steps of the National Palace. Spiders of sunlight shivered over their brass instruments. They wore royal blue uniforms with big brass buttons and coils of gold braid. There were about forty of them and they all looked like admirals.

There was a great cheer as four Cadillac limousines entered the plaza from the north. They moved at a funereal pace. You could not see anything through the tinted windows. Rockets were launched from the four corners of the square; there were prolonged whistles and parabolas of smoke, and then the rockets exploded into stringy flowers of red and yellow and blue.

The limousines halted in front of the palace. Lackeys rushed forward to open the doors. The American candidates, old Hamilton Keyes and Rachel Leah Valentine, exited from one of the limos; the four missionaries from another; and government big shots, in black silk suits and snappy military uniforms, emerged from the other two cars.

The band started playing the country's national anthem. Three fighter jets in close formation roared low over the square, rattling windows and churning the smoke, and when the noise of the jets faded I could again hear the music and the cheering crowd.

* * *

The President of the Republic welcomed the people, welcomed the liberated missionaries, welcomed the distinguished American political candidates, welcomed a new day of national reconciliation and international amity. The crowd applauded. The band played a lively *pasodoble,* "Cielo Andaluz," as if the president had just cut ears and tail from a bull.

The American vice-presidential candidate ended her speech with a series of rhetorical spasms.

"Now!" she cried.

"Ahora!" the dark-haired girl near her repeated in Spanish.

Feedback from the speakers situated around the square resonantly echoed the last syllable of each word.

"And tomorrow!"

"Y mañana!"

I crawled forward and propped the rifle barrel on the window sill.

"Forever!"

"Siempre!"

I placed the intersection of the telescope's crosshairs between Rachel's breasts.

"All of the people!"

"Toda la gente!"

"Everywhere!"

"En todo el mundo!"

The crowd loved her.

Rachel Leah Valentine arched her back, spread her arms wide and—ecstatic, cruciform—gazed up at the incandescent blue sky.

I gently squeezed the trigger.

Now. Let it all come down.

Printed in the USA
CPSIA information can be obtained
at www.ICGtesting.com
JSHW082203140824
68134JS00014B/393

9 781620 454268